# I AM THE PRODIGAL

## I AM THE ELDEST

BETTY SAWATZKY

I AM THE PRODIGAL, I AM THE ELDEST
Copyright © 2024 by Betty Sawatzky

Unless otherwise indicated, all scripture taken from the New King James Version®. Copyright © 1982 by Thomas Nelson. Used by permission. All rights reserved. Scripture quotations marked (NIV) are taken from the Holy Bible, New International Version®, NIV®. Copyright © 1973, 1978, 1984, 2011 by Biblica, Inc.™ Used by permission of Zondervan. All rights reserved worldwide. www. zondervan.com The "NIV" and "New International Version" are trademarks registered in the United States Patent and Trademark Office by Biblica, Inc.™

This is a work of fiction. Names, characters, places and incidents either are the product of the author's imagination or are used fictitiously, and any resemblance to actual persons, living or dead, businesses, companies, events, or locales is entirely coincidental.

Printed in Canada

Soft Cover ISBN: 978-1-4866-2480-5
Hard Cover ISBN: 978-1-4866-2482-9
eBook ISBN: 978-1-4866-2481-2

Word Alive Press
119 De Baets Street Winnipeg, MB R2J 3R9
www.wordalivepress.ca

MIX
Paper from
responsible sources
FSC   FSC® C103567

Cataloguing in Publication information can be obtained from Library and Archives Canada.

# INTRODUCTION

Prod·i·gal [ˈprädəgəl]
ADJECTIVE
1. characterized by profuse or wasteful expenditure: lavish
2. recklessly spendthrift
3. yielding abundantly: luxuriant[1]

The parable of the prodigal son is famous for revealing the deep love of a father for his two sons. Often we focus on the younger son, the prodigal, the one with the adventurous spirit, whom many of us can relate to. He is the son who insulted his father by asking for his inheritance early. He shamed his family and the entire community knew what he had done!

However, due to his own desperation, only after the money ran out did the young son return home, willing to work for his father to pay back what he had squandered. The father welcomed him back with open arms and no conditions. Though the prodigal son had foolishly squandered his extravagant inheritance, the father celebrated in extravagance upon his return.

Many of us can relate to the eldest son, the son who stayed home and worked faithfully by his father's side. The oldest son lived daily in the extravagance of his father's house, but rather than being excited *with* his father upon the return of the younger

---

[1] "Prodigal," *Merriam-Webster*. Date of access: September 21, 2023 (https://www.merriam-webster.com/dictionary/prodigal).

brother, he was angry *at* his father, refusing to accept his younger sibling back into the family. He accused his father of outrageous wastefulness in the celebration of the youngest's return, even suggesting that his father was foolish in his extravagance.

Both sons failed to see the heart of their father. Both were focused on their own desires and opportunities. Each felt they had the right to be in their father's good graces. The eldest felt he deserved his father's favor through obedience whereas the youngest felt he deserved his father's favor by demand.

What many of us don't realize is that the story goes much deeper. Jesus was speaking directly to the Jewish priests and scribes who stood firmly for the rules and laws of the Torah. They had been watching Jesus interact with prostitutes, tax collectors, the homeless, the sick, and the poor... the "sinners" who needed Him. The temple leaders were appalled at the extravagant love Jesus offered these people, freely and without conditions. The Pharisees resembled the eldest brother, feeling that they deserved God's favor through their dedication and fierce enforcement of the rules and traditions. In turn, they felt that the poor and lowly, the "sinners," deserved no chance of salvation; they had made their choice of reckless living and deserved to be in the state they were in... lost. Yet the Pharisees were just as lost, if not more so!

This book shares the story of the prodigal son, but with an examination of the culture and customs of biblical times. Once we understand this culture, we will better understand the extravagance of the father—and then we will better understand the extravagance of our heavenly Father and His Son, Jesus.

## JESUS TELLS THE PARABLE

Now the tax collectors and sinners were all gathering around to hear Jesus. But the Pharisees and the teachers of the law muttered, "This man welcomes sinners and eats with them."

Then Jesus told them this parable: "Suppose one of you has a hundred sheep and loses one of them. Doesn't he leave the ninety-nine in the open country and go after the lost sheep until he finds it? And when he finds it, he joyfully puts it on his shoulders and goes home. Then he calls his friends and neighbors together and says, 'Rejoice with me; I have found my lost sheep.' I tell you that in the same way there will be more rejoicing in heaven over one sinner who repents than over ninety-nine righteous persons who do not need to repent.

"Or suppose a woman has ten silver coins and loses one. Doesn't she light a lamp, sweep the house and search carefully until she finds it? And when she finds it, she calls her friends and neighbors together and says, 'Rejoice with me; I have found my lost coin.' In the same way, I tell you, there is rejoicing in the presence of the angels of God over one sinner who repents."

Jesus continued: "There was a man who had two sons. The younger one said to his father, 'Father, give me my share of the estate.' So he divided his property between them.

"Not long after that, the younger son got together all he had, set off for a distant country and there squandered his wealth in wild living. After he had spent everything, there was a severe famine in that whole country, and he began to be in need. So he went and hired himself out to a citizen of that country, who sent him to his fields to feed pigs. He longed to fill his stomach with the pods that the pigs were eating, but no one gave him anything.

"When he came to his senses, he said, 'How many of my father's hired servants have food to spare, and here I am starving to death! I will set out and go back to my father and say to him: Father, I have sinned against heaven and against you. I am no longer worthy to be called your son; make me like one of your hired servants.' So he got up and went to his father.

"But while he was still a long way off, his father saw him and was filled with compassion for him; he ran to his son, threw his arms around him and kissed him.

"The son said to him, 'Father, I have sinned against heaven and against you. I am no longer worthy to be called your son.'

"But the father said to his servants, 'Quick! Bring the best robe and put it on him. Put a ring on his finger and sandals on his feet. Bring the fattened calf and kill it. Let's have a feast and celebrate. For this son of mine was dead and is alive again; he was lost and is found.' So they began to celebrate.

"Meanwhile, the older son was in the field. When he came near the house, he heard music and dancing. So he called one of the servants and asked him what was going on. 'Your brother has come,' he replied, 'and your father has killed the fattened calf because he has him back safe and sound.'

"The older brother became angry and refused to go in. So his father went out and pleaded with him. But he answered his father, 'Look! All these years I've been slaving for you and never disobeyed your orders. Yet you never gave me even a young goat so I could celebrate with my friends. But when this son of yours who has squandered your property with prostitutes comes home, you kill the fattened calf for him!'

"'My son,' the father said, 'you are always with me, and everything I have is yours. But we had to celebrate and be glad, because this brother of yours was dead and is alive again; he was lost and is found.'" (Luke 15:1–32, NIV)

# CHAPTER ONE

## *The Road*

Aziel yanked hard on the reins, hoping to take the donkey by surprise, to catch her off-balance and make it move her feet again. It didn't work. The animal arched her neck and snorted stubbornly in front of him, all four feet firmly planted. She lifted her head, eyes bulging frantically, and released a terrified bray out of her foaming mouth.

"Bayesh! You stupid donkey!" screamed Aziel. "I should have sold you when I had the chance. I don't want to be here either, but you need to move so we can get out of this place."

The donkey hopped backwards with a kick, violently shaking her head and ripping the reins from the young man's hands. But Aziel was quick and grabbed the donkey's halter. He held on tight with one hand, almost losing his balance on the gravelly road as the animal jerked her head again.

Aziel detected movement to his left. As he turned to face it, he noted two figures coming towards him along the narrow road, the steep rockface rising behind them.

Bayesh brayed again, sensing the danger closing in on them. She stepped back with a start, almost dragging Aziel with her. He kept his tight hold on her halter, not wanting her to wrestle free from his grip.

The leather strap bit into his hands as he spied the two men. He desperately needed to get off this desolate road to somewhere safe, anywhere but here. They were too vulnerable! He had expected heavier traffic on the road, but so far he hadn't encountered many people. This stretch of road was the ideal place for thieves to wait in hiding for their chance to jump unsuspecting travelers.

The two strangers were getting closer now, the man in front taunting them with a toothy smile. He had a crooked nose and sagging cheek with a deep scar, clearly the lasting results of broken bones from a previous fight.

Aziel stumbled back in alarm as he saw a third figure slip out from behind a rock along the deep ravine, below which death awaited anyone who stumbled over the side. Panic gripped him as he eyed the three figures. He had a knife to protect himself but had foolishly packed it away with the rest of his possessions on the donkey's back.

*Why did I take this road?* he groaned inwardly. *They warned me not to come this way, but I wouldn't listen.*

Eyeing the approaching men, he took note of their ragged garments and unkept appearance.

"Look, I don't want to cause any trouble," Aziel called out as he grappled with the harness to turn the animal around. "I just want to pass through. I mean no harm!"

Aziel scrambled up onto the animal's back, but the donkey skittered to the side and bolted forward. He landed on the ground with a thud and a cloud of dust, the breath knocked out of him.

By now the three men were standing around the frightened young man as he gasped for air.

"You're making this too easy!" The leader, and also the oldest of the three, nudged Aziel roughly with his foot, then broke out into laughter.

The other two snickered along.

"Now, what is a lonely traveler doing on a road like this in the evening hours?" mused the second man, hooking his pudgy fingers on rounded hips. The words dripped with sarcasm. "Don't you know it's not safe to travel alone? This road has been known to attract some very dangerous men. Men who could kill you and take all your belongings!"

Another roar of laughter erupted between the robbers. The third man stared down at Aziel with steely grey eyes and spat on the ground beside him, just missing his head. The man wiped his nose on his sleeve.

Drawing a ragged breath, Aziel attempted to scramble onto his feet but the man with the grey eyes kicked him down just as fast.

Aziel reached for a nearby rock, anything to defend himself with, but the act only brought down the heel of the man's foot on Aziel's hand, grinding his fingers into the gravel. He heard the crunch of bones and cried out in pain.

He managed to roll himself into a standing position as he held his bloody hand close to his body. "You can't treat me like this! I'm not just some simple peasant. I'm the son of..."

A peal of laughter burst out of the leader's mouth as he bared brown and broken teeth. "I don't care whose son you are. Why, you could be the son of Ceasar Augustus himself venturing out to conquer and raid for your rich papa!"

He threw back his head and laughed again. The other two bandits joined in the chorus.

"I have no money, no silver, no gold, not anything," Aziel stammered as he tugged his cloak around his shoulders. "Just let me pass."

The tall, scraggly-looking man standing to Aziel's left side cocked his head. "For someone who has no money, you're wearing some very nice clothes. You know, we could fetch a healthy price for that cloak. And your sandals haven't walked many miles either."

Aziel looked around nervously, spotting Bayesh to his right near the rocks. She was too far away.

"Look, I don't have time for this. Get out of my way." Aziel waved his hand impatiently and started to walk around them, feigning control of the situation.

The leader stepped to the side and bowed deeply. "I understand, my lord, but we have some unfinished business with you."

The flash of the man's blade caught the evening sun.

Aziel thought quickly. There were only three of them. If he went down, he wouldn't do so without a fight.

He made a run for Bayesh, taking them by surprise, but within three steps he was tackled from behind. He kicked furiously, catching the tall one in the knee. The man crashed down on top of him with a shriek.

The leader leapt atop Aziel with knife in hand and plunged his blade deep into Aziel's left calf. His senses reeled as a cry escaped his lips, but weighty fists pummeled his head. He tasted blood in his mouth as his teeth slammed together from another blow. A foot to his back knocked the breath out of him, followed by another kick, this time to the gut. Then a blinding blow to the side of his head sent him into a spinning, inky blackness. He fought desperately to stay conscious, but the abyss was all-consuming, pulling him in…

The leader dropped the rock from his hand and mopped the sweat from his sagging cheek. He reached down and tore the cloak from Aziel's shoulder and stripped him of his tunic.

The stockier of the three men snatched the sandals from their victim's limp feet and tossed them to the tall man, who was already hobbling towards the donkey, standing in the shadows of the towering canyon wall.

With one last satisfied grin, the two men picked up Aziel and tossed him over the edge of the ravine. His lifeless body rolled down the rocky canyon, slamming against a wall of granite with a sickening thud.

Blackened hands that hadn't seen water for weeks grabbed ahold of the donkey's halter. The grey-eyed man scrambled as best he could onto her back, resting his swollen knee against her flank. With a switch to Bayesh's backside from a leather strap, the three men began their descent down the road to the region of Kadesh, hooting at their injured companion and newly acquired possessions.

### Azekah

Weary brown eyes scanned the horizon for any sign of movement. Gamaliel's aging face, weathered from time and worry, drew into a grimace, his mouth tight, hidden behind a greying mustache and grizzled beard. He sat at a table, staring longingly out the window towards the road. The house was positioned on a hill overlooking the village of Azekah.

Under Gamaliel's watchful eye, the community slowly awoke with the rising sun. The bright ball of fire was just peeking over the hills, casting gentle shadows over the Valley of Elah. Soon the town would be bustling with activity—goods being sold at the market, hearty greetings exchanged between neighbors, and jovial laughter shared over stories of the day before.

The village was fortified by a five-foot stone wall, and over it he could easily see the road which led into town. It was the only road into Azekah.

With trembling hands, Gamaliel brought the cup of hot tea to his lips and sipped. He was searching, waiting, longing to see a lone figure walk along that very road towards the gates. Maybe today would be the day his son returned to him.

His heart ached as he remembered their last conversation. It had been more of an argument.

"I want what is rightfully mine," demanded the young man, his brown eyes bright with insolence. "I don't want to live anymore under your rules, under your authority. I need to live my life the way I want to—to see what's beyond those hills, to experience other people, other lands, to taste adventure and really live it!"

Gamaliel had known this day would come, when wanderlust would enchant his youngest son to the point that no amount of persuasion or warning of danger would change the boy's mind. He loved his son, but Aziel had no idea what was beyond those hills. The world could be cruel to an impetuous young man aching to see it, ready to throw all caution to the wind.

Yes, Aziel's adventurous spirit could get him into trouble. Gamaliel and his wife Ednah had seen it many times in the brief eighteen years since the boy had been born to them.

Anan, their oldest, was often exasperated with his younger brother for taking life so leisurely. Anan was a hard worker, a very serious fellow, and always had been. But Aziel loved to engage in horseplay and hijinks. He was always up to some scheme to make people laugh—to make anybody laugh, for that matter. His great sense of humor is what made the boy delightful to be around. And at the same time, infuriating.

Gamaliel remembered their son—a child in a man's body, really—on the day he had stood before them, accusations and demands spilling out of him. It had felt like the boy had one foot stuck in foolish desires and grandiose dreams, but he demanded a man's respect though adulthood still seemed years away.

"I'm sick of being told what to do," he had spat at his father, his voice deepening with emotion. "I'm not like Anan, yet you keep expecting me to act like him, to work like him, to be serious about everything. I want to do things my way for once!"

Gamaliel and Ednah had looked at each other, bewildered at this eruption.

"Father, give me my portion of the inheritance. It belongs to me."

The ache in Gamaliel's chest had been immediate. That inheritance should only have been his after Gamaliel had died. He didn't know what to do. Should he give Aziel what he wanted or deny him? Should he stand by and watch his son leave the safety of his family and community with empty pockets and no means of securing food or shelter?

Either way, he would be losing his son. Whatever decision he made, it could result in Gamaliel never seeing him again. At least with some resources, the young man had a chance to survive.

With a broken heart, Gamaliel had sold a portion of his land, land that had been in his family for generations, and given it to Aziel. To lose part of one's land was to lose part of oneself. It represented a major loss of honor and respect in the community as well. His young son didn't realize that he was asking his father to tear his very life apart. And along with the land, Gamaliel had given him one-third of the sheep in the paddock, one-third of the cattle in the pasture, and one-third of the goats. It was a tremendous loss, but that was his son's inheritance—one-third of everything he owned.

To Anan, the oldest son, he gave the remaining two-thirds, as was the tradition of his people.

It had taken only a few days for Aziel to sell his portion of the livestock to neighboring farmers. He then gathered his belongings and loaded up the donkey, Bayesh, and walked away from the village of his birth with a skip in his step and not a care in the world.

Gamaliel and his wife had stood at the top of the hill and watched their son walk down the road and out through the gates with a determined stride. They'd watched as he disappeared down that dusty road into the blue-tinged hills of Elah, blossoming with the flowers of wild lupines.

"Will we ever see our son again?" Ednah had asked.

The question caught in her throat and Gamaliel's heart broke as a sob escaped her lips. He couldn't answer, for he too felt the painful ache of sadness... the anguish of rejected love.

Gamaliel was startled back to his seat at the kitchen table, sipping tea as his wife swept into the room, holding two round loaves of bread, freshly baked from the stone oven outside.

"You're deep in thought," she said.

He turned to her. "Yes... yes, I am," he answered, taking another sip of tea as his eyes scanned the hills through the open window.

## CHAPTER TWO

### *The Ravine*

The roar in Aziel's ears was deafening as he slowly opened one eye. He had to blink a few times to clear his vision. His left eye was swollen shut from the blood that had congealed from the gash on the side of his head. Judging by the blazing sun that beat down on his bruised and bloody body, it must have been afternoon. Every part of him that had been left exposed to the scorching rays was now sunburnt, raw, and blistering.

His stomach churned at the excruciating pain of trying to move his legs. Tears filled his eyes from the sheer exertion. His left leg was twisted under him and he knew it was broken. His calf burned hot and he faintly remembered a blade penetrating his muscle, although he had no way of knowing just how deep the wound extended.

He turned his head to the side, getting a look at his injured hand and tried moving it. His fingers were disfigured, bloody, and swollen; they were probably broken as well. His whole body was battered and bruised from being tossed into the ravine like a worthless sack of broken clay pots.

Closing his eyes, he tried to remember what had happened. It was all a blur. His last memory was of his tunic being torn off his shoulders and the sound of Bayesh braying loudly, mixed with the sound of laughter...

Aziel opened his eyes with a start, forcing that second eye open, if only a slit.

He needed to get moving, to get out of here, to somehow climb up that steep ravine. Hot tears of shame rolled down his face as he wept. He had been such a fool, and in so many ways. His father had warned him of the dangers potentially hiding behind every wall and rock, on every road. But no, he hadn't listened.

Aziel closed his eyes, trying to blink back the stinging tears.

"I've been such a fool," he mumbled. "I just wanted to live my life to the fullest, without stupid rules and restrictions. Look where it led me, from one disaster to another."

He lifted his head, wincing as he pushed himself up to take in his surroundings. His body was pressed against a huge boulder. When he tried to move, though, the left leg wouldn't budge at all and a sharp stab in his calf took his breath away. Waves of nausea churned in his head and he hurled violently.

He held himself as the vomit spilled down his chin. His injuries were too great. He was going to die in this place if he didn't get some help. But was it wise to call out? Would that bring the robbers back to finish him off? Would anyone even hear him?

The sound of footsteps on the road high above him interrupted his thoughts.

"Hello?" he called out weakly. "Is anybody there? Somebody, help me please!"

It hurt to breathe, and even more to call out, but after a moment the footsteps stopped.

"Help me please," he cried again.

The sound of footsteps continued on.

"No… please don't leave…" he called, louder this time. "Please, help me! I'm down in the ravine!" He coughed out, gasping with pain. "Help me…"

The footsteps quickened their pace and soon faded away.

"Don't leave... please don't leave," he sobbed. "I need help... please..."

Aziel hurled again, his body contorting with each painful retch. Then the inky blackness swallowed him up once again. The pain was too great...

## Azekah

Anan glowered as he spied his father walking solemnly down the path towards the village gates. He reached into the bag of grain that was strung across his torso, grasping another handful of wheat to throw at the ground.

"Every day he watches and waits, or sits and waits, or works and waits... it's pathetic," he sneered. "He's forgotten what's important—the family he has right in front of his eyes. And there's work to be done. So much work to be done! It's just pathetic."

Anan was the oldest brother and, in his opinion, the wisest and most hard-working of his entire family, especially now that his father was so preoccupied with his brother's departure. Since Aziel had demanded his share of the inheritance and left, their home hadn't been the same. Their family was the brunt of every joke in the community, the subject of conversation around their neighbors' tables and whispers of gossip in the village market. All talk was of this wayward brother of his, Aziel the prodigal.

"Why, if he was my son, I would have slapped his face and sent him on his way, disowned!" one neighbor had scoffed.

"Slapped?" said another. "I would have beaten him within an inch of his life!"

"Asked for his inheritance? I would have said, 'Ask for mercy for your life!'"

"Or how about, 'You want to leave? Don't ever think of coming back!'"

Many had busily surmised where the young scamp had gone, or how he must be spending the fortune he'd been given. Some even concocted stories of Aziel landing himself in prison. He was too nice a boy to land in prison for something as serious as murder or robbery, but maybe he'd gotten himself into trouble for having an affair with a nobleman's daughter. He was a handsome young man, that was true, and he did have lots of money to spend!

Others suggested he might have accumulated deep gambling debts and been forced to sell himself as a slave to pay it off.

At least the kindest of the townspeople proposed he had become a wealthy merchant and lived in a big house with many servants.

But the consensus was that he must have squandered his inheritance in the company of fellow gypsy-travelers, with his loose living and insistence on answering to no one.

Anan hated being the subject of village gossip. It was humiliating enough to watch his brother embarrass himself and his family, but why had his father allowed one of his own children to disgrace him in this way? A son asking for his inheritance before his father's death was the greatest insult any father could bear. It was like wishing his father dead, and now Gamaliel would carry the shame of it to his grave.

Not only would such a family disown the delinquent son, but the entire community would shun him. Such a child would never be welcomed back. If he dared return, he could be stoned to death.

"It just makes me sick," seethed Anan, sweeping the dark curls out of his eyes as he reached into the cloth bag again and threw another handful of seed onto the freshly plowed dirt. "Aziel the fool takes off with a fortune without a thought towards how his selfish ways will affect everyone else. And now all this work falls on me..."

His father was distracted at all times of day, watching the road that wound its way through the distant hills to the gates. Their mother silently wept and prayed, then wept and cooked, and then wept again. It was like she floated from room to room in a daze, not knowing what to do with herself. This vibrant woman who had once loved to sing and cook and sew and tend to the garden and laugh with friends and family... well, she was nothing more than a somber and silent shadow of herself.

"I hope he's destitute. He deserves it for destroying our family..."

Amidst the muttering, he went about sowing wheat. The workers helped him tend the land, but he was furious with his parents, especially his father, for leaving him with the bulk of the farmwork. His father had too much compassion whereas Anan had none. At times he still caught the look of disappointment in his father's eyes, or the look of hopeful expectation. Anan would just turn away, averting his father's gaze. He knew what the looks were all about; it was supposed to be Anan's responsibility to go after the wayward brother. Being the oldest, he would normally be given the larger share of the inheritance so he could take care of the family when their father passed away. It was his duty to bring his younger brother back home.

But this was a very different set of circumstances. Their father was very much alive!

Still, Anan frowned to himself. He couldn't help but feel a pang of guilt that he was partly responsible for the family's grief. Aziel had made his own decision to leave. Being the eldest son, and now the only son on the farm, Anan needed to take the lead at home, not run after his impetuous little brother.

The guilt only stirred up greater rage. Aziel had left with plenty of money and possessions. What matter was it whether he was alive or dead? Anan didn't care. Besides, perhaps Aziel was doing well, like a few villagers suggested. Perhaps he owned his own house or had bought a business and become a wealthy merchant...

Squinting into the afternoon sun, he put his brother out of his thoughts. Aziel had humiliated them all by choosing his own road.

"He's dead to me," he breathed, forcefully throwing another fistful of grain to the ground.

# CHAPTER THREE

## *The Ravine*

Aziel clawed his way out of the heavy blackness that kept trying to pull him back. The pounding in his ears was deafening, making it difficult to sort out the sounds around him. A long, lonesome howl mixed with the sound of lapping water. Something wet tickled his face and a tongue licked his forehead. He felt pressure as something tugged at his open wound. Teeth nipped at the raw skin and hot, putrid breath fanned his face.

Then he heard the sudden snarl and snapping of teeth, awakening his senses and dragging him towards consciousness. Panic mixed with confusion as he realized he was no longer alone in the ravine.

He snapped awake, feeling the ominous presence of the creature slinking around him, lapping up his vomit, howling that doleful cry from the depths of a hungry belly.

He was surrounded by wolves.

## *Azekah*

Gamaliel sat at the village gates, watching the hillside for any sign of his young son. It had been months and still no sign of Aziel.

The morning sun was warm on his face, but the sadness in his heart was almost unbearable, so much so that even a beautiful day couldn't lighten his mood. He had no way of knowing for certain whether his beautiful son was alive and well, or if he was dead. The world could be an ugly place, merciless and cruel.

He remembered years ago being a young man, with much the same spirit as Aziel. He'd been caught up in his own grandiose dreams and wanderlust. His adventurous spirit had eventually lured him away from the sanctuary of his family and community.

A shadow crossed over Gamaliel and he looked up to see Reuel, an elder of their village, making his way towards him, his body hunched over from years of work tending to fields and livestock. The elderly man groaned a little as he sat on the stone bench next to Gamaliel, grasping his walking stick with thin, gnarled hands. He squinted his eyes as he stared far off into the distance, creating deeper crevices in his aged face.

Reuel had lived in the village of Azekah all his life, having been born and raised there and then establishing his own family. His wife had passed on many years before. His two daughters were married and had blessed him with more than a dozen grandchildren, many of whom now had children of their own. Both of his daughters helped to care for him now that he was approaching his mid-nineties.

Gamaliel greeted Reuel with a nod, but he had no words to share. His heart was too heavy for conversation. He couldn't even manage a casual greeting.

The two men sat in silence, staring out at the hillside as they watched the sun rise higher in the azure sky over the valley. They had a commanding view from their perch as the sun shone on the tiniest droplets of dew, creating delicate diamonds that shimmered across the rolling hills.

"Yes," said Reuel quietly. "The valley of the terebinth, where our forefathers camped when King David fought the mighty Goliath…"

Gamaliel nodded, recalling the story of that great battle between David, the young shepherd boy, and the Philistine giant. It was one of the most amazing stories told by their grandfathers. The Philistines had camped on the southern side of the valley, with King Saul's army occupying the north. At the bidding of his father, David had travelled the twelve miles from Bethlehem that day to check on his brothers, camped on the northern hill. It was there where he saw the enemy calling out to them to fight, the challenge led by Goliath himself. Young David had known the power of his God, Jehovah, and chosen five smooth stones from the brook of Elah, at the heart of the valley, in preparation for battle against the great and terrible giant.

Gamaliel thought of how greatly young David had depended on Jehovah to protect him. Was Jehovah protecting Aziel now? He noted the difference between the two young men; one had followed God's ways while the other followed his own.

Reuel cleared his throat and spoke slowly, trying to hide the waver in his voice. His words were thick with emotion. "If you remember, Gamaliel, I too lost my son to the call of those hills... I too know of that ache in your heart, that chasm in your very soul that cannot be filled with anything or anyone other than your child, longing to hold him in your arms once again... a hollow so deep that at times it feels like it will crush the living breath out of you." Tears rolled down the old man's weathered face, "Yes, I know that ache, Gamaliel."

Gamaliel swept a tear from the corner of his eye and wiped his nose on his sleeve. "Did I do wrong in letting him go? Should I have fought harder for him to stay? I taught my sons to live in wisdom and make good choices... to work hard so the land rewards you... to take care of your flocks and herds... I knew Aziel was an adventurer, but this? This cold disregard for his family?" He turned to Reuel, deep creases etched around his eyes. "This intentional turning away from his people? This brazen demand for his share of the family's farm and livestock? My heart is broken, Reuel." He sighed, remembering the sight of his son walking way. "My heart is broken…"

"Our sons are warriors at heart, and we were there once too." The old man smiled as he recalled his own years of sowing wild oats. "The world seems to be encroaching on our families, on our morals and ideals. It's a different world in some ways, yet the calling of unrighteous living has always been there, from the time of Adam and Eve biting into that fruit to the time of Noah and the horrific flooding of the world. It is still there today."

Gamaliel merely nodded.

"It seems our generation of sons have another word for 'unrighteous living.' *Adventure.* That seems to justify their actions," continued Reuel. "Yes, all men are warriors at heart, needing to conquer new lands, needing to prove themselves as men. Not to us, but to themselves. Both of our sons felt the need to conquer the unknown world that lies over those hills."

Reuel inclined his head out towards the valley.

Gamaliel turned to face his elder. "I understand. That's why I let Aziel go his own way. He is free to do as he chooses. I couldn't force him to stay, couldn't force him to *want* to stay. What hurts is that he wanted his inheritance, his portion of generations of hard work, more than he wanted me. I don't want him to be forced to love me, Reuel. From his love for me should spring desire, respect… a servant's heart! That's what I want for both of my sons."

Gamaliel breathed deeply as he thought of his oldest son, Anan, who had obeyed his wishes, but not always with a giving, loving, or tender heart. More and more, Gamaliel sensed a distance growing between them, a coldness that he couldn't explain or understand.

"Jehovah led David to this very valley to face the giant that threatened our people," Gamaliel murmured. "Perhaps Jehovah will lead my son back to this valley, back to my waiting arms."

A long silence followed as the two stared out across the distant hills, now fully bathed in the light of the morning sun.

At last Gamaliel turned to the older man. "Do you still miss your son?" he asked quietly.

"Yes," Reuel whispered. "His loss tears at my heart. I don't know where he is, or if he is even alive. He could be just over that hill, close to home, and I would never know it. I fear I will die an old, old man, never to see my strong, handsome son, Halal, ever again."

# CHAPTER FOUR

## *The Ravine*

Aziel's hand searched for a sizable rock he could use to ward off the wolves circling around him and pawing at his limbs. He struck the snout that was nearest his face, resulting in a yelp, a scuffle, and then a menacing growl. That growl grew louder as more joined in on the growing threat.

"Get away from me!" He swung his arm in the darkness. "Get out of here!"

The animals seemed keen on this interaction and stepped closer. Curiosity turned into determination; growls turned into snarls. They seemed to prefer their meal to be a fresh kill, rather than a rotting corpse.

"Leave me alone! Get out of here!"

With renewed strength, Aziel raised himself and shuffled into a sitting position, with his back against the boulder. His head throbbed with every movement and the pain in his left hip and leg proved almost more than he could bear. He threw the rock with his good hand and scooped up a second one just as fast, holding his broken hand against his chest.

"Get away! Get away from me!"

His screams were met with vicious snarls.

A slip of a moon gave little light, illuminating only the movement of shadows around him. He frantically squinted into the darkness and made out five or six animals. It was only a matter of time before they overtook him. He had seen it enough times in the field when a lone wolf snuck into the paddock and got the sheep moving, chasing the flock until one stumbled from sheer exhaustion. In only a few moments, the wild would overtake the innocent, weak and breathless.

He sensed more wolves closing in on all sides. The little strength he had waned quickly and the stench of his own blood and shredded flesh was thick in his own nostrils. The pack would know this, and that he would make for an easy meal.

"Get away!" He screamed and kicked at the teeth that nipped at his bare foot. "Leave me alone!"

Emotion and exhaustion, pain and weakness, overwhelmed Aziel and he broke into heaving sobs.

"I'll kill you if you come close! Go away! Get away!" Thinking of the horror he was soon to experience, being torn apart by hungry wolves, he held his hands to his chest and cried in desperation. "Jehovah, my God! Please take me... just take me now. Please help me! Don't let me die this way..."

Suddenly the ravine lit up with the orange glow of fire and a shout from the road above.

"Get away!" yelled the voice. "Get away, I say!"

A man was sliding down the shale embankment with a torch, the fire casting contorted shadows across the massive boulders. The wolves turned their full attention to the oncoming figure and the man shouted again.

"Get away! Get out of here!"

A few of them leaped to the side and into the darkness, but three wolves remained, their heads lowered, shoulders hunched, ready to spring. The man screamed again and waved the blazing torch side to side to ward off the beasts. One got scorched and howled as it bowled over the other.

The man waved the torch again and jabbed it at the last remaining wolf. It turned quickly and scampered into the night.

The stranger jammed the flaming torch between two rocks and knelt beside Aziel. The dancing flame cast a glow on the young man propped up against the huge rock.

"I see you're hurt. Can you walk?"

"I… I don't know," stammered Aziel.

Steady hands touched his head and gently lifted his matted, blood-crusted hair. As the stranger got a better look at the head wound, Aziel settled back against the boulder. He closed his eyes, groaning, and tried to relax against the rock, but his body began to shake violently. The excruciating pain in his hip and leg confused his thoughts and gnawed at his senses.

He opened his eyes again and spied the sandaled feet that stood beside him… the footwear looked odd… from a different land…

The last thing Aziel heard was the tearing of cloth as he slumped forward into the man's arms. He was once more consumed by the sickening blackness…

## *Kadesh*

Attilius stepped carefully along the rows of green shoots that peeked out of the dirt. It was the growing season, but the summer rains hadn't yet come. By now the sprouts should have been at least five fingers tall, but they were only two or three at best. He looked up into the sky, shielding his eyes from the blazing sun, his strong jaw clenched in deep thought. There wasn't a cloud to be found. Not even a wisp of white.

He shook his head and looked down at his feet, studying the parched ground. The entire area, once lush with healthy crops, had turned into a dry and thirsty land. From its lofty location, the village of Kadesh commanded an expansive view over a richly varied landscape of fields and hills dotted with the large, shady terebinth trees that kept watch like sentinels.

Attilius stood just over six feet tall, a commanding presence. He continued his walk around the field, eventually turning onto the path that led up to his family's house just outside the village. He would carry more water to the field that evening when the temperature was cooler. Under the current intense heat, the sun sapped up any moisture it could find; pouring water onto the tender leaves would scald rather than revive them.

His wife, Cloelia, would have the noon meal ready. As Attilius made his way up the path, he smelled the fresh baking waft from the open windows. There was nothing like the smell of fresh bread to warm the hearts of men! This brightened his mood and lightened his step as he quickened his pace up the path.

A middle-aged man wearing stained and ragged clothes met him. He was carrying the slop pail but stepped aside, allowing Attilius to pass on the narrow trail. Attilius acknowledged his worker by nodding, then carried on. The worker greeted him back, briefly, before resuming his lumbered walk behind the barn, limping awkwardly while carrying the heavy pail.

"Papa!" a girl's voice called out.

Young Cassia ran from the barn. A brown, scruffy looking mongrel ran happily beside her as they neared Attilius. The dog, Bean, was an eight-year-old mixed breed who held the girl's full attention, her very heart. The pup was the color of a kidney bean; when he'd been brought to their home, Attilius had been able to hold him in one hand. Now the dog was full-grown but still had the energy of that well-remembered puppy!

Attilius chuckled at the sight of them, Cassia and Bean. They made quite the pair!

"Papa!" she called again, her cheeks flushed and blue eyes sparkling. She ran up to meet him, breathless with excitement.

"Sunset had her babies, and she had twins. Twins! Isn't that amazing? Come and see. They're so cute. I love them! Come and see!"

She grabbed his hand and pulled him towards the barn, chattering away. He laughed aloud. His Cassia had always been a chatterbox, right from the day she'd realized she could make noise.

Sunset was the girl's nanny goat, named for the soft brown patch on the animal's side; it was formed in the shape of an arc, reminding them of a sunset. Each year Sunset would provide a baby goat, but this year she had given birth to two.

They entered the barn together, Cassia almost skipping as she pulled her father along. Once inside, she put her finger to her lips and smiled up at him, meeting his blue eyes with her own.

"Shhh," she whispered, not wanting to disturb the nanny goat, who was bonding with her babies.

The two little ones were ambling around the pen awkwardly while their mama gently licked them. One flopped over and into the straw. Cassia laughed, then clapped a hand over her mouth with wide eyes, realizing that she'd startled the goats with her sudden noise.

Bean looked up at the girl, panting happily as if laughing at her sudden outburst.

"Well, look at that," said Attilius with a smile. "They both look strong and healthy. So have you named them yet?"

Cassia named all her pets, even those animals that weren't pets at all.

Bean pushed his nose up into the man's hand, looking for a friendly pat. Attilius glanced down and grinned at the mutt. He remembered when the neighbor had brought the pup to their door, having been blessed with a whole litter. Cassia had gathered little Bean into her pudgy five-year-old arms and hugged him closely.

"You remind me of a little bean," she'd said. "I'm naming you Bean!"

Now, at thirteen, she was just as passionate about all the animals on their farm. She pointed to the baby goat curled up against the stall wall, nestled in the straw.

"That one is mostly white, so I'm calling her Snow," Cassia said. "She looks like she came down from the mountains, where the snow lays. Just like in the stories you tell me, Papa." She gestured to the second kid, gingerly suckling its mother. "That one has brown patches all over, so I'm calling him Patches. I was going to call him Blotches, but I like Patches better!"

Attilius laughed at his daughter's explanation as a breathless woman appeared at the barn door.

"Here you are," the woman exclaimed. "I thought I heard talking in here!"

Attilius smiled at his wife. Cloelia was as beautiful as the day he had met her some twenty years earlier. He chuckled at her appearance. She was hot and sticky from baking bread, and her hair was unkept; it looked like a loose halo around her head. He winked at her.

"Mother, I was just showing Sunset's little babies to Papa." Cassia squealed, only to clap that hand over her mouth again and giggle, her mischievous blue eyes dancing.

"I thought so." Cloelia chuckled. "It's time to come in now. The bread is freshly baked and the stew is hot."

Attilius reached for his wife's hand as they made their way out of the barn and walked towards the house. Cassia ran up to join them as Bean trotted beside.

"Now Bean," said the girl, wagging her finger at the mutt. "If you behave yourself, you might get a bit of stew or a bite of bread."

Each member of the family took turns washing their hands in the pail of water that stood on the table against the house's exterior wall, beginning with Papa.

Cassia shared the particulars of Sunset's birth of the two kids, right down to the afterbirth, to which she scrunched up her face while describing the gory details. She had known enough to stay out of the pen unless the mother goat was having trouble; then, of course, she would have had to call for her papa's help.

Both Attilius and Cloelia smirked at Cassia's explanation, which became quite graphic. She waved her hands animatedly as she described every detail.

They soon followed inside the tantalizing smells of the kitchen and sat at the table. Cloelia spooned thick chunks of vegetables into wooden bowls, placing them in front of her family. The freshly baked bread had already been cut into wedges and positioned in the middle of the table.

Suddenly, Bean jumped up and faced the open door, barking incessantly.

"Bean, stop that!" yelled Attilius.

He rose from his chair and strode out the door to see what had caused such a disturbance. Bean was always quick to respond to intruders.

A portly man was walking up the path to the house. Bean followed his master outside, barking louder. When Attilius yelled at the dog again, it prompt Cloelia to call the dog back in.

The dog turned but stopped short of the door and glanced back to the path, more threateningly this time. Despite this, the heavyset visitor made his way up the well-worn path, his walking stick pacing him with each step.

Cloelia recognized the man at once.

"Bean, come here! Come here now!" she commanded.

When the dog didn't stop, she motioned for Cassia to help her take him to the bedrooms at the back of the house. Bean growled and Cloelia held him back, although it took everything in her not to let the dog go. She almost wished the mongrel would take a good bite out of this visitor's ankle.

"Keep him away," she said firmly to her daughter as Cassia took the dog into the bedroom and shut the door behind them.

Attilius led the visitor into the house.

"Well, looks like I'm here just in time!" the man said. "Fresh bread and stew! I could smell it from down the road."

"It's been quite some time since we've seen you around here, Balbus," Cloelia said in a cool voice, eyeing him suspiciously. She did her best to act cordially and hoped the two men wouldn't notice her contempt. "What brings you to our home?"

Attilius happily pulled out a chair for the barrel-chested man to sit at the table. "Uncle Balbus, come and join us!"

"Why, thank you, nephew," drawled Balbus, his jowls bouncing as he looked up at his nephew's wife. "Cloelia, it's so good to see you! You get prettier every time I visit. And I'm sure your lovely daughter is looking more and more like you every day." He looked around the kitchen. "But where is little Cassia? Have you married her off yet?"

Cloelia glanced nervously at her husband.

The middle-aged man rubbed his belly, threw back his head, and laughed jovially at his own remark. Attilius joined in the laughter and handed Cassia's bowl of stew to his portly uncle.

# CHAPTER FIVE

## *The Ravine*

Elihu lifted the young man he had rescued onto the donkey's back and steadied him. He had wrapped his own cloak around the bruised and battered man before hoisting him over his shoulders to climb the steep ravine. Carrying the man proved difficult, as his feet kept slipping out from under him on loose rocks and stones. Meanwhile he held fast to the torch, both for light and to keep the wolves at bay. The wolves had kept their distance but watched carefully should the two men come tumbling back into the ravine.

He promptly set the young man on his donkey's back and wrapped the rope snuggly around the man's waist and the animal's neck.

Elihu now looked more intently at his new companion's face. It was difficult to guess his age in the dark, even with the glowing light of the torch, but he seemed about eighteen years old and not much older. He was more a boy than a grown man. What had he been doing out here on this lonesome road all by himself?

It was no mystery how he had landed himself in that ravine. His injuries looked to be the result of robbers catching him unawares. He was lucky to still be alive. His wounds were fairly fresh, meaning that this had happened over the past day or two. His skin was damaged by bruises, gashes, and sunburn. He was not in a good way. Any longer and the wolfpack would have made a meal out of him.

Once Elihu secured the knot, he gently coaxed the donkey forward, walking more beside it than in front, in case the injured man's weight should shift and he slip off. He had dressed the deep wounds as best he could, finding a strip of cloth from his pack to wrap around the man's head after cleaning the gash with fresh water. The leg was most certainly broken, maybe even the pelvis; it was hard to tell in the dark. And that gash to his calf was deep and still oozing. The right hand had been damaged as well. It looked like it had been stomped on, breaking the tiny bones in the palm as well as all four fingers. The face, too, was badly bruised and swollen.

Elihu managed to coax a few sips of water between the man's swollen lips, which briefly revived him before he slipped back into unconsciousness.

The nearest village was about fifteen miles away, and Elihu estimated he would reach it by midmorning. The moon was now a gentle grey as the sun prepared to rise, casting soft shades of pink and purple across the horizon. Oh how he loved the mornings and the palette of colors that adorned the start to each and every day. Jehovah created masterpieces upon the canvas of the sky countless times a day, but His sunrises and sunsets were simply breathtaking!

"The heavens declare the glory of God," he breathed in awe, lifting his eyes to the shifting colors above. "The skies proclaim the works of His hands!"

Elihu spotted the humble village below, nestled in the hills. He looked forward to visiting his dear friend and his wife. The innkeeper Manej was a gentle man, a good man, and his wife Marta was compassionate and caring.

Yes, Elihu would bring this young fellow to the innkeeper's house and pay for his stay as long as was needed. It would take a number of weeks, most likely months, for the wounds to heal. Rest in a clean bed, along with hearty meals, would help the boy to recover, albeit with some ugly scars to show for his ordeal. The innkeeper and his wife would help him get back on his feet. They would be a blessing to him on his journey.

Elihu strolled through the village gates, leading his donkey by the reins and keeping careful watch over the young man who still rested against the animal's neck. The villagers welcomed him warmly. Some waved and others greeted him with a smile. Elihu answered back with a greeting and a wave.

He made his way through the winding street and stopped in front of the innkeeper's house.

As Aziel slowly awoke, he felt the warmth of the sun on his back. He felt the rocking sensation underneath him as the animal shifted its weight from side to side. He lifted his head and peered from behind swollen eyelids to see the stranger speaking with an older gentleman in front of a house. Aziel could not make out what was being said as their voices mixed with the sounds of people passing by. He heard the faint ring of coins bumping against each other in the palm of the older man's hand.

The stranger now stood to his left and untied the rope that held him in place. Strong hands guided Aziel off the donkey's back and carried him through the front door of the house and into a back room. He was laid gently on a bed and covered with a blanket.

He slipped into a feverish sleep as gentle hands carefully washed his face. The inky blackness began to envelop him again…

"I'm so sorry," he whispered. "I'm so sorry…"

"I know, Aziel," said the stranger. "I know. Just rest. You're safe now."

## *Azekah*

Reaching for another fistful of flour, Ednah rolled the dough between her hands, kneading it forward to back, then side to side. She preferred to bake bread every day, but the joints in her hands were getting stiffer from the changes in the weather. Some days her left thumb locked up with a painful muscle cramp, and she would be down to one hand to finish preparing the loaves for the oven.

She swept a wisp of greying hair away from her eyes and glanced out the window. Her husband Gamaliel and their son Anan would be returning from the market later this afternoon, so the loaves needed to rise and bake in time for the evening meal.

She finished kneading her dough, divided it into four round loaves, and placed them on four separate platters. Then she went to the doorway and called out to their servant.

"Tomas! Would you help me with the bread please?"

Within minutes, a middle-aged man, rather short but lean, answered back and joined Ednah in the kitchen. He knew that his master's wife struggled with lifting platters of heavy dough up onto the windowsill and was happy to help. He promptly lifted each one and placed it in the sunshine to encourage the yeast to rise.

"Thank you, Tomas," said Ednah with a gentle smile.

He smiled back at her. "Is there anything else I can help you with?"

"No thank you, Tomas. This will be fine."

Gamaliel had promised to bring home dried fish from the market, as well as freshly picked pomegranates. Figs and olives would round out their meal, as well as the freshly baked bread dipped in olive oil.

She tidied up her kitchen and placed the cloth bag of flour up high on a shelf with the salt and yeast.

Aziel had always loved her baking. She couldn't wait to see his bright, handsome face when he rounded the corner and excitedly took her in his arms and whisked her around the table in a silly dance.

She laughed to herself. Aziel had always taken great delight in teasing his mother!

But wait. Aziel wouldn't be surprising her from around the corner today, or combing his tanned fingers through his curly hair as he usually did when his black locks tickled his face. He wouldn't smell her fresh bread or cup her face in his hands and kiss her on the nose. He wouldn't wink at her when peeling off a corner of the loaf, just minutes before the others came through the doors.

From the day Aziel had left to chase his dreams of adventure, the house had been quiet. Very quiet. She remembered him on those days, days that seemed so long ago now, skipping up the path to share the latest news he'd heard at the market, or the hilarious stories that made him laugh. That rich, infectious laugh could light up the room. Or he would tell them of something that had caught his attention or aroused his curiosity. Other days he would question his father and older brother to better understand a concept that didn't make sense to him. He was inquisitive, that Aziel!

But he'd always reserved that winning smile for her, and often the antics that accompanied the smile made her laugh out loud.

And then there had been those times when he shared his heart, his hopes and dreams, his troubles and worries, while wrestling with daily life and a developing conscience that made him question people's intentions. He would shake his head in bewilderment at what others said and did to one another. She often sat at the table with him and helped him find a solution to some dilemma, or helped him see a situation from another's perspective.

The last day she and Gamaliel had seen him, she'd hugged him and held him close, not wanting to let go. She had kissed him on the collar bone. He had grown so tall! And with tears in her eyes, she had told him that she loved him, and that she would be praying for him.

He'd cupped her face in his hands, as he always did, and kissed her on the nose. He had smiled at her with that beautiful smile, those deep brown eyes twinkling at her.

"I love you too, Mother. Don't worry, I'll be careful. And I'll come home to you, not to worry."

Ednah wiped her hands on her apron and looked down with a sigh. It had been months since Aziel had left, but the ache in her heart was as fresh as though it had happened yesterday. It had been said that a mother could only be as happy as her saddest child. She had no way of knowing if her Aziel was in a good way, whether she should be happy or sad. She just knew that he wasn't with them, and that alone caused her to grieve. She offered up a prayer for her son, for Jehovah to protect him and lead him home to his family.

# CHAPTER SIX

## *The Innkeeper's House*

Marta's weathered hands mopped the feverish brow of the young man who had been brought to their home. Their friend Elihu had brought them another traveler who had been attacked and left for dead on the side of some road. Her husband, Manej, had helped Elihu carry the man into the house. Then she had proceeded to tend to his wounds. The infection in his leg had already made itself known by the time he'd been brought to their door.

Now, three days later, he was still ill. The fever needed to break soon.

The leg wound was slowly changing from a swollen, bluish tinge to red and raw. It looked very ugly, but there were signs of positive change, even if slight. It was the fever raging through his body that she worried about. They could lose this young man.

Marta dipped her cloth into the bowl of cool water on the little table beside the bed and wiped his face and forehead again. Although he was quite swollen, the bruises on his face were changing for the better.

He mumbled something unintelligible, but she couldn't understand. She squeezed his hand, trying to soothe his restless spirit as he slipped into a feverish sleep, haunted by his memories of the past few months.

## The Tavern: Four Months Ago

Aziel leaned up against the counter in the little tavern where he had spent the past few days. It was a happy place where everyone was everyone else's friend! He tossed a few coins onto the counter, thanked the burly tavernkeeper behind the counter for his drink, and then turned to face the room, which was lively with music and dancing and laughter.

The musicians in the far corner were a straggly-looking bunch who kept everyone's spirits high with the lilting of pipes and flutes and timbrels, keeping time with the constant beat of a drum. The tambourine player was especially animated as he danced; he shook and slapped his instrument with practiced hands.

Yes, in this place every day was a celebration—and it was exhilarating!

Skirts drifted this way and that as three women danced in the middle of the tavern, their movements intoxicating. But only one woman caught Aziel's gaze as she spun and twirled in a red and purple skirt that flowed around her legs. Her black hair hung loosely around her shoulders, shifting with each movement of her arms. Her blouse was a soft creamy white that accentuated her smooth, olive-colored skin. He couldn't tear his eyes away; her beauty captivated him as she glided with the rhythm.

Glancing in Aziel's direction, she noticed the handsome young man watching her. She swayed between the tables to dance before him, her mouth curled in a seductive smile, flashing perfect white teeth. She held his gaze with her eyes, a bewitching green that sparkled from behind thick, black lashes.

She reached up and ran her fingers through his wavy mop of hair, gently tugging at a curl. She then turned and danced her way back towards the center of the room, all the while able to feel his stare boring into her back.

The men sitting at a nearby table erupted in boisterous laughter. One of them threw up his hands and shook his head in defeat.

"I give up!" he howled. "Today is not my lucky day."

The others jeered, trying to persuade him to go just one more round.

He laughed raucously. "No, you scoundrels. You've convinced me too many times. Soon I'll be walking out of here in bare feet… with not a slip of silver to my name! My wife will have my head. I'll be out sleeping on the roof tonight, to be sure."

The room erupted into fresh peals of laughter as he slowly stood and ambled away, his senses dulled from too much drink.

Aziel broke away from watching the dancer, his eyes focused on these men having fun at their companion's expense. As he observed them, the group coaxed Aziel closer.

"Why don't you take a seat?" one of them asked. "Join us."

Aziel sat and smiled around the table expectantly. He was quite familiar with the game of casting lots. He and his older brother had played it all the time when they were boys to see who would tend to the cattle that day, or sheer the first sheep in the spring, or haul the water from the well, or distract their wily rooster while the other collected the hens' eggs. One stone per player was placed in the cup. Then it was shaken and each person retrieved a stone. White stones were winners. The one holding the sole black stone would have lost.

Aziel had been watching the various tables play over the past few days. They were letting "the gods" decide who would pay for the next round of ale.

He rubbed his hands together with an eager smile as he swept his eyes around the table. "So, who has the cup?"

A swarthy man with a saucy smirk that tickled the corners of his wide and mustached mouth squinted at Aziel from under thick bushy eyebrows. Not taking his eyes off the new arrival, he pushed the wooden cup to the middle of the table with one large hand.

"You start," he grunted smugly.

# CHAPTER SEVEN

## *Azekah*

The morning air was scented with the sweet fragrance of freshly picked fruit mixed with the earthy aroma of garden vegetables. The market bustled with the activity of people on the move to make their purchases, everything from fish and fruit, eggs and goat's milk, to blankets and household items, even tools needed to work the land and livestock.

Gamaliel greeted the neighbors who passed him and Anan with a hearty "Hello" or quick conversation. Anan stared straight ahead, not wanting to make eye contact with anyone along the way.

The two men stopped at the fruit stand to purchase a half-dozen pomegranates that Ednah had requested. Anan picked up one of the bright red fruits to inspect its smooth skin. He bounced it in his hand thoughtfully; it felt firm and of good weight, good indications that the seeds were full and juicy. But the fruit was marred and not quite ripe.

He set aside the perfectly rounded fruit, searching for ones with more angular sides. Those would be the ripest, ready to eat. He reached for another and turned it in his hand to look for cuts and bruises. Satisfied, he placed it carefully in his sack and reached for the next one, glancing nervously at the townspeople mulling around them.

Gamaliel greeted the vendor warmly and placed two silver coins into her hand. "Good morning, Betany! Your fruit looks as delicious as always. We'll purchase six pomegranates please. Ednah has plans for a special dish this evening."

Betany smiled back. "I'm sure it will be wonderful. Your Ednah is a wonderful cook and baker! My husband wishes I could cook so well... but then he would be a bigger man than he is already!" She chortled. "With hungry men to feed, I'm certain your kitchen is always busy, and your oven always warm."

Anan's eyes twinkled at the woman, who stood about a foot shorter than him. "Mother keeps herself busy in the kitchen, keeping our bellies full." He chuckled as he placed four more fruits in his sack to complete the half-dozen.

"Anan, you seem to grow taller every time I see you," she chided. "You have most certainly grown taller than your father. And so handsome!" She turned to Gamaliel and leaned in. "You and I must both be getting shorter."

The two men happily agreed and bid her farewell.

They walked casually through the square, Gamaliel briefly stopping to chat with this vendor and that neighbor, enjoying the village chatter as he did every morning. Nearby children played with a makeshift ball made of rags of cloth rolled and tied together. They laughed and hollered at each other as they punted the ball around the legs of the people in the market.

Gamaliel was purchasing dried fish when the scene was suddenly broken by hollering to the south. The sound disturbed a flock of chickens that set to clucking and cackling excitedly.

"I've found him! I've found my silly little lamb!"

It was Shimon the sheepherder. As the man made his way down the street, he tugged on the lamb's dainty legs straddling his neck. The animal looked stained and spent, as if it had put up a ferocious fight with something twice its size. But Shimon looked in worse shape! His clothes were torn and his feet muddy. He had scratches on both legs and the sleeves on his tunic were spotted with crimson.

"It took many miles of searching, but my lamb is back here with me, safe and sound," he bellowed from his sun-weathered face. Blisters were starting to form on his burnt nose. "Come, friends and neighbors! Celebrate with me, for I have found my lost sheep."

Shimon's whoops and hollers brought folks to their doors and windows to see what all the commotion was about. The adults gathered around and the children stopped playing. As they listened, he shared his ordeal, a story of how the silly sheep had wiggled itself out of the paddock, eager to reach a patch of greener grass just a few feet from the pen. Its aimless munching had led it so far away that it couldn't find its way back.

"It was caught in a bramble bush and couldn't move," Shimon explained to the crowd. "A twig was caught in its wool and there it stayed! The poor thing was so tired of fighting with the twig that it flopped right down there on the spot. That very spot! Didn't you?" He chuckled as he gently stroked the lamb's legs. "I was sure the wolves would get you, my silly little Umbaa. Yes, I know you by name, you mischievous bumpkin who smells greener grass and follows your nose…"

The man glanced up at the sweet face peering at him with sleepy eyes.

"I was up all night looking for you, Umbaa," he went on. "I searched the paddock. I searched the creek. I looked in the bushes and under trees. I left my entire flock just to find you. You! And there you were, caught on that little twig in the brambles. But here you are now, back with me… yes, back with me. Let's go home, Umbaa!"

Shimon waved to the townspeople and once again invited them to join him at his home for a celebration. He then continued down the street, singing and laughing. It seemed the celebration had already begun!

As the crowd dispersed, Gamaliel and Anan looked at each other gravely. Without saying a word Anan turned and walked away from his father lowering his eyes to the path in front of him. He made his way towards home. A sense of guilt nagged at his conscience. His brother had ruined yet another start to yet another day, and Aziel's name hadn't even been mentioned.

Fixed in front of the fish vendor, Gamaliel watched his eldest son leave his side, walking through the crowd away from him. He turned to see the procession of people trailing after Shimon. He was uncertain of what to do. He would be expected to join the others, but he was reminded too painfully of his own lost sheep, the one lured by the greener pastures of other lands. And his oldest son seemed to be lost as well, in his own way.

He felt an arm drape around his shoulders, the warm embrace of his old friend, Reuel. The two men watched the lively crowd follow Shimon around a corner and out of sight. In the distance, they also saw Anan slowly make his way up the hill to the courtyard in front of the family home.

No words were needed. Both men understood the ache in each other's heart.

The two men then turned and walked away, Reuel making his way to his own street and Gamaliel following in his oldest son's footsteps. He proceeded up the path to their house full of memories, with an empty chair on one side of the table.

## *The Tavern: Four Months Ago*

The shortest and roundest of the men eyed Aziel with a smirk tickling the corners of his wide, mustached mouth.

41

"I haven't seen you in here before. Where are you from?" he asked sweetly. His swarthy hand reached around the table, gathering up the stones to drop them again into the wooden cup.

Aziel glanced around the table, all eyes on him. "I've been here for a few days now. I like this town. I think I'll stay awhile."

The wooden cup was shaken vigorously and each man took their turn retrieving a stone from it.

Aziel reached in, feeling confident in himself. He studied his companions. What were the odds? There were seven men around the table, so he had only a one in seven chance of pulling the dreaded black stone. The odds were in his favor, but he didn't fancy the idea of paying for the round of drinks. He had lots of money, so that wasn't a problem. It's just that he had a list of all the different cities and regions he still wanted to visit. His inheritance needed to last for more than a few months.

Aziel pulled his hand out of the wooden cup and showed the crowd his find—the black stone. He flashed a fake smile, trying to hide his disappointment.

The room erupted with a roar. "He pulled the black stone, he did!" someone hooted.

"Let's do it again," a second man jeered. "Give him another chance!"

"He's new to the game! Let's go another round!"

Each man plopped his stone back into the wooden cup and the entire room fell quiet. Even the musicians held their song and lowered their instruments, watching intently as the cup was shaken and each man pulled out a stone as the cup travelled around the table.

Aziel was the last to retrieve his stone. He held his breath, waiting to dip his hand into the cup and watching each one as they held their stones tightly in their hands.

The swarthy man slowly opened his hand, the cue for the others to follow suit. Each one revealed a white stone... leaving only the black one in the cup for Aziel.

He had lost another round.

The room erupted into even louder disorder than before. Fists pounded on the table and feet stomped wildly as the men convulsed in fits of laughter. One of the men slapped Aziel briskly on the back.

Aziel's face was hot with embarrassment. But he smiled bravely and cheered, as boisterously as he could muster, "Drinks for everyone!"

The patrons spurred him on as the tavernkeeper started to fill empty cups. The musicians started up their song and the dancers twirled in the center of the room again.

The swarthy man glanced at Aziel as he retrieved the stones for another round, then raised a bushy eyebrow. "I've heard about you. You're the one who's come into quite a sizable amount of money, yes?"

"Yes," Aziel sputtered, surprised by the question. "I've received my inheritance and decided to see the world for myself. Live life to the fullest!"

He beamed, lifting his cup of ale with enthusiasm.

"Well, we're sorry to hear of your father's passing, but we're thrilled you're sharing it with us," the man crowed, slapping both hands on the table in front of him. He turned to the tavernkeeper. "Keep the ale coming! And it's on our new friend."

Aziel's eyes widened. He laughed as he pushed his cup forward to knock against the swarthy man's own, sloshing ale over both their hands.

"To life!" he cheered, licking the ale off his grimy fingers.

## *The Innkeeper's House*

Steady hands unwrapped the bandages on the young man's left leg, revealing a gash that still oozed a mixture of pus and blood. Marta brought the bowl of warm water up onto her lap, squeezed out the cloth's excess water, and began gently washing the wound. His fever hadn't broken yet, and she was worried he may not survive the infection raging through his body.

The injured man stirred as she continued to run the clean water over the angry wound. Eventually she dried off the skin to let it breathe before applying a new poultice.

With fresh herbs, mixed with crushed figs, honey, and mud, she prepared a paste handed down to her from generations past. Honey served as an antibiotic agent and the earth's naturally rich minerals would provide healing. Altogether the paste would increase blood flow to the wound and draw out the pus.

She carefully stirred the concoction with hot water and spooned it onto a clean square cloth over the gaping wound. She held it with one hand and wrapped his leg with a long strip of cloth to hold it in place.

The unconscious young man jerked his leg, irritated at her touch. She stopped, waiting for him to settle, then continued on. He flinched again, groaning as he tossed his head to the side.

The bandage around his head was stained with a patch of blood. His head wound had started to bleed again. She would need to tend to that next.

### *Azekah*

Gamaliel reached for his wife's hand as he spoke the blessing for their evening meal. It was a practice they had started from the first day of marriage. At each meal, their hearts united to thank Jehovah for His provision, for the blessings of the day, and for all they had. They also lifted up their struggling friends and neighbors.

But Aziel, their youngest son, was the greatest petition they could bring before the Lord. They prayed he would be safe from harm and come home.

This prayer made Anan uncomfortable. His parents always held hands when they prayed, but pleading for his younger brother at the foot of Jehovah's heavenly throne was like asking the Creator to bless a wolf that eyed a flock of sheep for its own gain. What was the sense of that? And why would Jehovah listen to their prayers, never mind respond in the way they felt He should?

*Foolishness,* Anan thought to himself as his parents ended with "Amen."

Gamaliel reached for the bread and broke off a chunk, dipping it into a small bowl of olive oil in the center of the table. An uncomfortable silence settled over the evening meal.

Ednah glanced between her husband and her son. "Thank you for the fresh pomegranates, Anan. They're perfect. Nice and juicy! And the fish was freshly dried as well. Thank you, husband."

She smiled at them both and the men mumbled their appreciation.

Ednah reached over and patted her son's hand, beaming. "I went for a walk to look at the crops, Anan. Each field looks so bountiful! It will be a very good harvest this year."

She watched her son bite into the chunk of bread he held in his hand. He had been a handsome son, and over time had grown into a well-muscled version of his father. His dark curly hair fell in waves almost to his shoulders.

"Thank you, Mother." Anan smiled briefly. "Yes, the crops look very good. We shall see what the next few weeks bring."

Gamaliel nodded, glancing up at Anan between bites. "Jehovah has blessed us with the rains and the heat in perfect order. You have done well, my son, in tending the fields."

Anan mumbled his thanks and lowered his head to eat solemnly.

Ednah turned excitedly to her husband, hoping for more lively conversation. "Was there anything new at the market today?"

The two men stopped eating and glanced at each other.

"Shimon lost one of his sheep yesterday," Gamaliel drawled between bites. "He looked everywhere and finally found it caught in a bramble bush." He took a slow bite of the fig in his hand. "He invited the entire community to celebrate with him…"

Ednah caught the increased tension between the two. Anan had glanced over at the empty chair beside him, where his brother would have sat. His sad brown eyes then swept over his parents. Slowly, he stood up and walked out of the kitchen.

Ednah stared after her son… this son who also seemed so very far away.

Gamaliel lowered his face. There were now two empty chairs across the table.

CHAPTER EIGHT

## *The Tavern: Four Months Ago*

The woman swayed with the music, keeping Aziel's eyes locked on her own, her skirt a soothing swirl of scarlet and violet. It was thrilling to watch! The flutes and timbrels followed the beat of the drum, drowning out the raucous laughter around the tables.

He was enraptured by those stunning green eyes, intoxicated by her beauty. She floated towards him, her eyes fixed on his. Then she reached for his hand, pulling him slowly up from his chair. She drew him close, wrapped her arms loosely around his neck, and moved her body into his. She kissed him on the lips, a slow, pondering kiss that drew the very breath out of him...

Soon he was being led to a back room, the woman guiding him by the hand as the music played. The drum syncopated behind him and he lost himself to this world of pleasure...

### *Azekah*

Gamaliel worked silently beside Anan, skillfully sweeping the scythe side to side as sheaves of wheat fell in a heaping row. He stood and mopped the sweat from his forehead with his sleeve. It was late morning and getting to be a scorching day, but the conditions were perfect for the harvest.

Anan glanced up at his father, then straightened and stretched to loosen his stiff muscles. "What do you think, Father? This is a healthy crop, I'd say."

Gamaliel smiled, feeling so very proud of him. His son had tended to the crops all summer with great care. His efforts and dedication had resulted in a healthy yield.

"The crop is thick and full." He reached up to squeeze his son's arm. "Yes, the harvest is very good. Good job, my son. Good job!"

A shout from one of the workers interrupted them, and Anan made his way towards the worker in the middle of the field. Gamaliel watched Anan walk gingerly between the sheaves of grain, admiring his son's growing wisdom and determination. He was embracing his role as a farmer by making knowledgeable decisions. He had grown quite tall, a striking man with broad shoulders and that same curly mop of black hair as his younger brother...

Gamaliel wondered about Aziel. What was he doing? Where was he? It had been many months now. Was he enjoying life just as he'd dreamed? Had he found the adventure he had sought?

Perhaps so. And perhaps he was on his way home.

Gamaliel gazed across the hilly landscape towards the road that led into the village. He squinted against the afternoon sun. What was that? A movement from far away at the mouth of the valley caught his attention. It was a lone figure walking towards the village along that very same road.

Could it be? Had Aziel come home?

Gamaliel dropped his scythe and dashed to the edge of the field, reaching the grassy pasture. He planted himself on the paddock wall, heaved his legs over to the other side, and bolted, weaving between the scattering sheep.

He stopped briefly to catch his breath. He knew he couldn't run very far, or very fast, but a light jog brought him through the

village and to the open gates. He continued through to meet the
man walking up the roadway.

"Aziel!" he called out. "Aziel, is it you, my boy?"

### Kadesh

Cloelia smiled at her daughter, who sat on the floor with an armful
of kittens. Cassia picked up the grey bundle of soft, downy fur and
cuddled the kitten in her arms, gently stroking its cheek.

"You and your animals," Cloelia said with a laugh. "If it's not
Bean, it's the chickens or Sunset and her little ones. And now
kittens."

"Oh Mama, they're so sweet and so soft! Do you want to hold
one? Here, hold this one. I've called her Sparkles... because her
eyes just sparkle."

"Right now I'm counting the money your father brought me.
He was at the market this morning and sold three laying hens, as
well as five dozen eggs. With this, we should have enough to buy
the cloth to sew your new dress. You're growing so fast, Cassia, I
can't keep up! Soon you'll be wearing *my* clothes."

They heard a bark outside and Cloelia walked over to find
Bean standing at the door, panting. The startled kitten scrambled
out of the girl's arm, scratching Cassia as it struggled to get away
from the frightening mutt.

"Sparkles!" Cassia lunged for the kitten as it skittered under
her mother's feet and beneath the table.

Bean made a dash for the ball of grey fur, bumping Cloelia's
chair and the table leg in his haste. The coins scattered and spilled
onto the floor.

"Oh no," the woman cried. "Cassia, get Bean out of here! He's
making a terrible mess."

Bean had cornered the kitten at the far end of the kitchen.
The little furball had arched its back and sounded as ferocious as

it could, hissing and spitting, even clawing at the dog if it dared to come closer.

"Oh, Bean, you silly dog. Out! Get outside now." Cassia pointed to the door.

Bean seemed happy at the sight of this new furry toy. He looked up at the girl innocently with dancing eyes and a lolling tongue.

Cassia scooped the kitten into her arms and led the dog outside by the scruff of his neck. The other kittens had scattered by now, making their way behind wooden crates and clay pots on the floor.

She returned and closed the door behind her to keep the kittens in—and the dog out.

Cloelia was on all fours under the table. "I'll help you gather the kittens, Mother," she offered, dropping to her knees.

"It's not the kittens I'm looking for. It's the coins! Help me find them, Cassia. They've rolled all over the floor!"

Their nimble fingers plucked the silver coins from behind the table legs and those same crates and the pot. The kittens scampered left and right as the items were moved out of the way for a closer inspection.

Mother sat back down in her chair and spilled the coins from her hand onto the table. Cassia joined her and carefully placed her own collected silver pieces into her mother's hand.

"...twenty-one, twenty-two, twenty-three, twenty-four..." As Cloelia looked up into her daughter's eyes, the color drained from her face. "I had thirty-four coins before Bean bumped into the table. We're missing ten."

The hunt was on. The two got back down on all fours, searching every corner of the room.

"Here's one!" called Cassia as she pushed aside a container of olive oil. "And here's another one, behind the leg of the side table!"

Cloelia peered under the little footstool beside the door. "Here are two more!"

Two kittens were wrestling behind one of the wooden crates. They tumbled up against it in a rolling mass of black and white fur. When Cassia gathered them up, she spotted yet another coin.

Cloelia reached for the little rug that lay in front of a stool and lifted it to reveal two shiny coins. "Here's two more!"

Something had caught the little grey kitten's attention and he was pawing at it, making it flip and spin.

The girl laughed. "Sparkles found another one."

The two continued the search, carefully lifting one item at a time and setting it down to study the space.

"Got it!" Mother called as she lifted a rag, revealing yet another coin. She sat back down in her chair and started to count. "Thirty-one, thirty-two, thirty-three... Oh! There's still one missing." She turned to her daughter. "Cassia, please bring the kittens back to the barn. We need to sweep this floor without any distractions."

"Yes, Mother." The girl scooped each of the kittens off the floor and into her arms to carry them out. She closed the door quickly behind her to keep Bean out of the house. Bean followed Cassia happily to the barn, hoping to frolic with his new playmates.

Cloelia got back onto her hands and knees, again desperately peering behind every crate, jar, and table leg, but to no avail.

Cassia soon dropped down beside her. She focused closely on the cracks in the stone floor. But there was no sign of the missing coin. It was lost.

"We need to start again," instructed Mother soberly. "I'll take this side of the room, and you take that side. Let's lift all the crates and jars off the floor and onto the table."

Within moments, she had clambered back down on all fours to reinspect the floor.

"Where are you…" she mumbled to herself. "Where would you be hiding…"

She slowly made her way along the wall to the doorway, checking each dip in the floor, every crack and crevice.

Still nothing! She groaned inwardly. This was not good.

She bent over again and spied an area of the floor where she hadn't thought to look—under the door. And there it was, wedged in a crack between the floor and the doorframe.

"Cassia, I found it! It's here under the door." She tried to pry it out from between the stonework, but it wouldn't come loose. "Daughter, please bring me a knife."

The girl picked up a knife on the counter and handed it to her mother. But no amount of coaxing could pry the coin out from between the stones.

"No, this won't do. It's too thick. I need a knife for slicing fruit. Please, Cassia, bring me the smallest knife we have."

Cloelia opened the door to get a better view of the coin stuck between the stones. Bean was at the ready to jump back into the house, but Cloelia stopped him with her hand and a quick "No!"

She carefully slid the thin knife into position. Suddenly, it popped out! The silver coin rang as it bounced over the stone and rolled under the table.

"Quick, Cassia—stop it!"

Bean jumped over Cloelia's arm and raced towards the rolling coin, but the girl managed to leap under the table and slam her hand over the thin metal object rolling away—just in time.

"Got it!" she crooned, standing proudly and wagging her finger at the excited Bean.

"Oh, Cassia, I'm so glad we found it!" Cloelia hugged her daughter tightly and laughed. "Oh my, thank you."

Cassia hugged her back and plopped the coin lightly into her mother's hand.

"And what is going on in here?" intoned a deep, booming voice from the open doorway.

The two turned to see Attilius standing just inside the threshold, his hands on his hips and a wide smile on his face. He loved seeing his girls happy together. Cloelia and Cassia, the loves of his life!

"Husband, we found the missing coin," the older woman cheered. "Bean knocked the table and the coins scattered all over the floor. We gathered them up one by one, but there was one we just couldn't find—but we found it, right there under where you're standing. There it was! Come and celebrate with us. It's time for cake and berries with cream."

Attilius threw his arms around his wife and daughter and hugged them close as Bean began his song of incessant barking in the background.

"Looks like I came just in time," chimed Uncle Balbus from the doorway, patting his rounded belly.

CHAPTER NINE

## *The Innkeeper's House*

Aziel felt a nip at his leg and kicked violently. The wolves were closing in for their kill.

"Get away from me," he muttered. "Get away…"

The wolf sank its teeth into his leg. His skin was on fire! Another tugged at his arm, snarling at him. He lunged at the vicious animal with his fists pounding empty air. He struck out again, clipping one on the side of its head.

"Get away from me! Get away!"

When he kicked again, blood bubbled from the bite in his calf. He screamed again, gasping and convulsing into dry heaves…

"We must cool him down," called Marta, the innkeeper's wife. "Open the window. Quickly, Manej!"

Her husband yanked open the shutters to allow the cold night air to spill into the room. She pulled the blanket off Aziel's fever-ridden body. He was delusional, fighting off something or someone. He had even caught her in the face with one of his thrashing fists as she tended to his leg.

Manej jumped to her rescue to hold down the frantic man, binding his arms with his own.

"No, Manej, just leave him," Marta said. "Let him alone… he's going to hurt you! He's delirious."

The innkeeper was backing off when suddenly the young man sat up straight and glared at them with wild eyes, black with fever. "Get away from me!" His voice was thick, his eyes wide like a trapped animal. "Get away!"

Sweat rolled down his forehead and into his eyes. The salt stung like tiny daggers. He then erupted with a gasping roar, rubbing his eyes violently. The pain in his swollen face produced even louder groans. The pounding in his head was all-consuming... deafening! A sob escaped his mouth as he held his head.

Through glassy eyes, he stared at the innkeeper's wife, terrified. He gasped for breath, then sank back down onto the bed, exhausted.

The music and continuous drumming in his ears seemed to fade as the woman with the green eyes led him to the back room again. His eyes followed the folds of her scarlet and violet skirt as it swished and swayed before him, coaxing him to follow...

# CHAPTER TEN

## *Azekah*

Gamaliel ran out through the village gates, even though the traveler was still a fair distance off. The older man squinted eagerly, searching for any sign of familiarity. The man's size and stature was much the same as Aziel's. His hair was similar, too, curly although a softer color than his son's black locks.

"Aziel! Is that you, my boy?" he called out.

But he was met with disappointment as he realized this traveler was not his son.

"Good morning, Gamaliel," the stranger called from afar. "It's a beautiful day for a walk!"

Gamaliel felt confused and discouraged. This was certainly not his son, but he didn't recognize the stranger who had just called him by name. The older man came to a stop on the dusty road, looking perplexed.

"Good morning," Gamaliel said slowly. "I'm sorry, sir, but I thought you were somebody else…"

"Yes, your son." The stranger beamed a wide smile, his hazel-colored eyes twinkling. "Aziel! Yes, I saw your son a few weeks ago. He was having some trouble, but he's doing better now."

"My son? You've seen him?" Gamaliel quickened his pace to come closer. When they were standing in front of each other, questions spilled out of him in excitement. "Oh, happy news! Where did you see him? Are you sure it was Aziel? Please, sir, come to my home and tell us everything." He reached for the stranger's arm in haste. "Please come…"

"Why, yes, Gamaliel, I would love to share with you and Ednah how your son is fairing out in the world of adventures."

Gamaliel paused with surprise at the mention of his wife's name. The stranger motioned for them to continue walking together, though, so the two men started up the road side by side. They soon passed through the gates.

"And now you must tell me about Anan," remarked the stranger. "How is your oldest son?"

"Sir, how do you know Anan? And how do you know my wife's name? Do I know you?"

The man wrapped one arm around Gamaliel's shoulders and grinned. "Ah, my friend! Come, let us go up to your house and visit with your lovely family…"

The two trekked up the narrow path up the hill, chattering as they went. Gamaliel saw his wife, and their servant Tomas, standing in their courtyard, picking fresh lemons from a low-hanging branch of a tree. Tomas held the large basket for Ednah as she carefully placed the fruit inside it. Gamaliel waved at her joyfully, bidding her to come.

She stopped and watched them amble closer, her brow furrowed in wonder. Who was this stranger with her husband? She didn't recognize him, but he seemed oddly familiar… perhaps he was a friend of her sons…

### Kadesh

The portly Balbus reached over and patted Cloelia's hand warmly. "My dear, you do put on a feast! Attilius, if it weren't you, my nephew, I'd steal her away. And your lovely daughter… where is Cassia now? She disappeared so quickly. I want to see how much she's grown."

Their guest slurped up another mouthful of wine, swallowed hard, and then filled his cup with more from the jug, secretly squeezing Ednah's hand in the process and slipping her a wink.

Cloelia pulled her hand out from under Balbus's pudgy grip and backed herself away from the table. She reached to pick up the empty bowls from the meal as she glanced at her husband, who smiled at his uncle. He seemed to be enjoying the visit immensely.

Balbus always had a story to share of his travels. The latest was of how he had tricked his half-blind neighbor by selling him a half-blind mule! The mule had wandered into the other neighbor's yard and ate their garden clean through! The two men roared at the misfortune of the neighbor with the ruined garden and the perplexing mule.

When Cloelia put the last clean dish back onto the shelf, she picked up the slop pail standing in the corner, as well as a full bowl of stew for Cassia. She excused herself to the back room as her husband and his uncle wiped tears of hysteria from their eyes.

Cassia was sitting on her bed playing tug-of-war with Bean using an old rag. When Cloelia entered the room through the curtained doorway, she passed the bowl of stew to her daughter with a finger to her lips.

The two of them slipped quietly out the back door and skirted around the house away from the windows. They headed for the barn in silence with Bean trotting happily beside them.

Cassia knew to keep quiet so as not to alert the men in the house that they had snuck out, especially Uncle Balbus. Cassia didn't like him. He reminded her of the swine in her father's field, with beady little piggy eyes that were always watching her. She shuddered at the thought and reached for her mother's hand.

As they approached the barn, Cloelia noticed their farm worker lumbering his way up the back path.

"Halal, here you go," said Cloelia, handing him the slop pail. "Thank you."

He nodded his head and headed back down the path behind the barn.

Cassia watched him go. "Halal always looks so sad. Not like Uncle Balbus!" She shuddered again at the thought of their visitor. "I don't like Uncle Balbus. He scares me."

Her jaw set, Cloelia glanced at her daughter. She knew that her husband's uncle had his eyes on the two of them. She couldn't shake the sick feeling in the pit of her stomach. Her instincts told her Balbus wasn't to be trusted.

Equally concerning was the man's influence on her husband. Attilius was a good man at heart and cared deeply for his family, but he still adored his uncle. She felt helpless. Attilius seemed to be changing in ways she couldn't put into words.

She lowered her head to watch their steps along the path to the barn, deep in thought and remembering the many stories her husband had shared with her about his favorite uncle.

When Attilius had been just a boy and his father died in a boating accident on the Sea of Galilee, Balbus had taken him and his mother under his care. Ever since the day of that terrible storm, which had killed all three men aboard the boat, Balbus became the most important person in Attilius's life. He'd taken a keen interest in the boy and taught him many things about farm animals, working the land, and tending a vineyard and garden.

He had even taught young Attilius how to catch musht, a panfish that was delicious when baked. Balbus had withdrawn a single hair from their donkey's tail and tied a kernel of corn at the end, then taught the boy how to jiggle the bait just right, lightly tapping the river bottom with the kernel. With a sudden yank, they would snatch the fish out of the water. Attilius had gone on to teach Cassia that very same skill.

Yes, her husband had gone on many adventures with his Uncle Balbus, some that seemed to her precarious and even foolhardy. Attilius simply adored him.

It was concerning that her husband didn't see the unwanted attention his uncle gave Cloelia and Cassia... especially Cassia.

Cloelia gripped her daughter's hand a little tighter as she pondered these troubling thoughts.

## The Innkeeper's House

Manej sat outside their little house under the shade of the carob tree, watching the villagers pass him by. The heavy branches with their dark green, leathery leaves provided protection from the warm morning sun. A gentle breeze carried the sweet and pleasant fragrance through the air. The tree's orange-yellow flowers were very small, almost inconspicuous, but that fragrance could fill one's very soul with peace.

He breathed deeply, filling his lungs with the sweet scent, and felt the breeze on his face.

"There's a song in the wind, a melody in the rain, and the sweetest tune in the scent of a flower," Manej whispered to his Lord, closing his eyes in worship. "Each one sings Your praises in their own tongue. The scritching of the elusive cricket, the cheeps, chirps, and trills of the song thrush... and then there is the melodious woot-woot of the hoopoe, the comical little bird that ambles along the roadway, displaying its illustrious crown of cinnamon feathers dipped in black."

Manej chuckled to himself, then opened his eyes and smiled up at the sky.

"Yes, each one adds a voice to the chorus of alleluias that reach up to the heavens with their songs of praise," he said to himself.

"Jehovah, if I would dare question whether You are with us, I would need only lift my eyes to the beauty that surrounds me. Your presence is apparent from the tiniest blossom to the majesty of the golden eagle!"

## The Tavern: Four Months Ago

Aziel lifted his arm and punched the air. "Drinks for everyone!" he shouted incoherently while smiling proudly at the men sitting around the table. He glanced back over at the tavernkeeper behind the counter, waiting for the man to respond to his call.

Ignoring the boisterous request from the young drunk, the tavernkeeper continued wiping the inside of the clay mug with a worn rag.

Aziel turned full around in his chair to glare at the burly man. "Didn't you hear me? I want to buy my friends another round of drinks!"

The man paused for a minute, eyeing Aziel while rubbing his hand across a bristly chin. Then he continued his task of drying the clay mug, all the while watching the belligerent young customer.

Aziel slowly rose from his chair, mug in hand, using the table as a prop to lean against to gain his balance. The air was hazy with dust and the stench of ale and body odor permeated the room. He made his way awkwardly between the tables towards the counter, bumping into patrons along the way. He staggered forward and slapped his hand down on the stone counter, sloshing ale.

"Did you hear me?" Aziel demanded, this time louder.

The tavernkeeper raised his eyebrows and then leaned in to speak to the young man over the eruption of laughter from a nearby table. "First you pay your tab. Then I'll serve you."

"Oh!" Aziel responded with jerk of surprise and a step backwards. "I can do that!"

He reached for the leather pouch tied around his waist. It felt lighter than he remembered. He flipped the pouch upside-down and dumped its contents onto the counter.

The tavernkeeper stared as he slid three coins towards himself. "This doesn't even pay for the drink you hold in your hand! Pay up!"

Aziel looked confused at the tavernkeeper, then at the coins, and finally at the empty pouch in his hand.

"Huh," he grunted. He ran grimy fingers through his mop of greasy hair. "Where is all my money…? Maybe Bayesh can pay my tab." He chuckled, cheering brightly. "Yes! I'll go ask Bayesh, for she must have my money!"

He giggled to himself as he stumbled a few steps sideways and turned towards the door.

A tall, lanky man stepped towards Aziel between the counter and tables, then faced him with steely grey eyes. "Where are you going, my friend? You have a bill to pay before you leave." He spat on the floor beside Aziel's feet for added drama.

Aziel squinted carefully at the man, then boasted triumphantly, "I'm going to find my… my servant… Bayesh… to get this good man his money!" He giggled to himself again and then staggered backwards.

A healthy nudge to the side of Aziel's leg almost pushed the young man over, and he swung around to look down at a swarthy man sitting at a nearby table.

"I don't think you understand, my lord," the man jeered, bowing slightly in his chair. "We're not letting you leave until you pay your tab with the tavernkeeper."

"Look, I'm trying to pay the man! Just let me pass and I'll get him his money." Aziel's temper prickled with anger and exasperation. He turned to face the lanky man blocking his path. "Let me pass…"

"I don't think you have any money, you pompous little pus!" The swarthy man growled from the side, nudging his leg again, this time with a heavier foot.

Aziel caught his balance. With hot anger, he lunged forward, his arm raised to strike the smug face grinning up at him. He was met with twinkling eyes and a toothy smile. The scar on the man's cheek twisted awkwardly on a sunken cheek.

"Go ahead," the man sneered.

The room fell deathly still.

Aziel stopped fast, his fist still raised in the air. He glanced around at the roomful of patrons, each one staring at him. He caught the eye of the dancer, whose green eyes darkened. She slowly and ever so slightly shook her head as if to say, *Don't.*

A pair of strong hands from behind heaved Aziel off his feet and dragged him out the tavern door, tossing him out onto the road in a drunken heap under the scorching afternoon sun.

"Hey!" he yelled, pummeling the air with misdirected fists. "You can't treat me like this…"

He struggled to stand up, but a foot shoved him flat on the ground again. His face hit the dirt hard. A roar of laughter erupted behind him.

"You can't treat me like this," he slurred between dusty lips, spitting dirt. He lifted his arm in protest, but it fell heavily to the side.

Laying the side of his face on the hot ground, he closed his eyes.

*Just to rest for a little while,* he told himself.

But soon the heat of the day took its toll, beating down and smothering him to the point that he couldn't breathe. The ground felt like it was spinning, and he was falling, his body was burning up as though in the very fires of Nebuchadnezzar's furnace.

## *The Innkeeper's House*

Marta picked up the bowl of cool water and the rag that lay beside it. The young man's fever had finally broken during the night and now he slept soundly. She rested her hand on his forehead to check his temperature, then walked lightly to the front door to join her husband in the courtyard.

Manej was sitting under the carob tree enjoying the shade of the late summer day as people walked past and greeted him warmly. He liked to people-watch, to take note of what they were doing, who they talked to, which direction they went... It was a relaxing pastime, practiced over many years.

He smiled when his wife joined him under the tree.

"How is our young man doing?" he asked. "He had a rough night."

"Yes, but his fever broke and now he's resting quietly." She nodded, then added, "I'm so glad. He must have been through a terrible ordeal to have that many cuts and bruises, never mind that gash to the leg. The cut was very deep. It's no wonder it got infected. He has a long road to recovery, but he's stronger than he looks. With good food and rest, I think he'll be all right. His body will heal. We have yet to see how his spirit will heal from the trauma, though. He's been through a lot and I fear his spirit may be broken. Time will tell."

Manej patted her hand. "What he needs is to see the beauty that surrounds him. It'll lighten his spirits and give him hope. The heart can heal when it's able to recognize God's hand in the beauty all around. When the heart and the mind join together to recognize these blessings and be thankful for each one, that is what gives hope—a hope for a new tomorrow, a new beginning, a new road walking with the Lord."

He looked down his shoulder at his pretty wife sitting solemnly beside him.

"We will pray for Jehovah to reveal this to our young visitor, and to heal his broken spirit," he said. "Jehovah takes care of each one of us, in His own special way for our own special needs."

As if on cue, a little green bird landed on a nearby branch. It opened its tiny beak to release its beautiful song from deep inside. Manej watched the creature's dainty head flit from side to side, its bright red eyes almost glowing against a black mask of feathers. On its cheeks, a splash of aquamarine led to the tiniest lime green feathers at its throat.

"Marta, see the little green bee eater," he mused. "This delightful little bird! Jehovah has shaped each of its feathers, each for its own purpose. So too He has done with me, and with you." He smiled down to his wife. "And to the young man inside our home. Jehovah has shaped each of us for our assignment, for His unique purpose."

Manej lifted his face to the Lord.

"I am Your servant, Jehovah, my Lord," he cried out, lifting his hands. "And You are our Provider, our Sustainer, and our Song. So we pray this very thing for our young man. Whatever his story may be, we lift him up to you, to heal him of his affliction—his body, his spirit, his mind, his emotions, and his heart. May he walk closer with You more than ever before."

"Amen," whispered Marta. "Amen. So let it be, Jehovah, our Lord."

CHAPTER ELEVEN

## Azekah

Elihu pushed back his chair and stood, smiling at Gamaliel and his wife. "Thank you so very much for your kind hospitality. You are a wonderful hostess, Ednah, and a marvelous cook!"

"You are most welcome, Elihu. You're most kind." She gave him a quick hug.

Their new friend chuckled as he hugged her back.

Afterward, the two men walked to the door and continued outside and down the path. Ednah went to the table and collected the bowls of fruit and fresh cream, her husband's favorite dish—fresh cream poured over chopped figs, with a spoonful of pomegranate seeds sprinkled overtop and just a dash of cinnamon. He had been very pleased at how quickly she had prepared the dish for them and their guest.

She set the bowls down beside the remaining pomegranates that her husband and son had purchased at the market the day before. Her family knew that each time they visited the market, they were to look for fresh pomegranates, picked that morning, because they didn't ripen afterward and could bruise easily when ripe.

Yes, Anan was very good at choosing the best fruit, judging them by their size and weight, shape and texture, looking for any imperfections.

She remembered when her youngest, Aziel, was just a little boy, coming home from scripture school. He had run into the house breathless with a new nugget of knowledge he had learned that morning.

"Mother!" he had gasped. "Guess what Teacher told us today? A pomegranate is very special because the fruit is said to have six hundred thirteen seeds, which is the exact same number of commandments in the Torah. Did you know that? I bet you didn't know that! Can you help me cut one open so we can count the seeds in one? Please, Mother?"

Ednah laughed again at her memory of her sweet son. She sat at the table, still holding the fruit and pondered the differences in her two sons; one judged the outside of the fruit and the other was captivated with the inside. In some ways, that's how each one viewed the world around them. The oldest immediately saw the imperfections in others while the younger was intrigued by what was on the inside, what made people act the way they did.

Her eyes wandered to the window where the setting sun cast its dazzling reds and oranges across the sky. She followed the winding road that led away from Azekah and down through the valley of Elah.

All the while, her heart ached. Elihu had told them that he'd seen Aziel a few months back. He'd been in a difficult situation and Elihu had helped him. It was so very kind of this stranger to help their son.

But that was a few months ago. Where was Aziel now?

Tears welled up in her eyes. Oh, how she longed for her son, her beautiful Aziel. She missed the way his brown eyes twinkled when he teased her, and his black curls that were more messy than neat. Tousled, that's what his hair was. Always tousled! She laughed aloud and wiped the tears trickling down her cheeks.

The flash of his smile had always melted his mother's heart. From the first time she'd held him in her arms as a newborn, he had stolen her heart. He'd opened his eyes to gaze with wonder into her own. Just like that, she was smitten.

Oh how her arms ached to hold him again. Her heart broke each time she thought of him. It seemed like only yesterday when he'd left their home, the safety of his community, and the care of his family who loved him so much... who *still* loved him so very much. Did he think of them anymore? Did he miss them? Did her precious little boy miss her even a little bit? Did he think of all the silly times they had shared together? Did he laugh out loud at the memories?

Her heart sank. Did he care about them at all, his parents and his older brother? Did he still love them?

Gamaliel entered the room and sat at the table across from his wife. He saw that she had been crying and reached over, gently taking the fruit out of her hand. He cupped both of her hands in his.

He lowered his head and prayed, "Jehovah Raah, You are the Lord our shepherd. We pray that You will shepherd our lost sheep and bring him back to us." Gamaliel hesitated, then continued. "Jehovah Jireh, You are the Lord who provides. We depend on You and You alone for everything we have and everything we need. We ask that You provide for the needs of our Aziel as he is on this journey. Jehovah Shammah, You are the Lord who is there for those who long to behold You at the end of our days. We pray that You will be there for Aziel. Do what is necessary for him to come back to us..."

A gentle sob escaped Ednah's lips and Gamaliel softly squeezed her hands.

He continued. "Jehovah Sabaoth, You are the Lord of Hosts, for those wise and humble enough to have our battles fought by

You and Your angelic army. Jehovah Nissi, You are the Lord our banner and we choose to faithfully follow You. We pray that our son Aziel turns from his wandering ways. As You led our forefather Moses with a pillar of fire by night, and a pillar of cloud by day, out of Egypt and through the wilderness, please lead Aziel out of the wilderness he is in, and back to us..." Gamaliel caught himself. "Back to You, Jehovah."

Ednah lowered her head onto her husband's hands and wept. "Yes Lord," she whispered. "Yes, back to You."

"You are Jehovah M'Kaddesh, the Lord who sanctifies those who want to live a life pleasing to You, and that is what we wish for our son." Gamaliel's voice lowered with heartfelt emotion. "Only You can turn him around. Only You can draw him back. Only You can soften his heart. Only You can breathe wisdom into him. Only You..."

His voice broke and he allowed the tears to flow down his cheeks. He must go on.

"You are Jehovah Tsidkenu, the Lord our righteousness, to those who trust in You. And we do... we trust in You. We trust that You are meeting Aziel where he is, whether he is healthy and safe, or living a foolish life, or in trouble, or in a dangerous place... we trust in You. Lord, You are Jehovah Shalom, the Lord our peace. And so we rest in Your peace here tonight, recognizing that You are El Roi, the Lord who sees all. You know where our lost sheep is. You know the circumstances he is in right now and You are working in his life to bring him back to You—and please, Lord, back to us. Speak to him in a language he can understand." He groaned aloud. "Do what it takes to bring him back to You."

Gamaliel could barely breathe. His chest heaved with a stifled sob.

"You are Elohim, the strong and faithful One, the one and only true God," he concluded, gasping. His breath was thick with emotion. "Amen… and so, let it be."

"Amen," whispered Ednah. "Amen."

She pressed her face into her husband's hands and wept bitterly.

## The Innkeeper's House

Manej sat in his favorite spot, under the carob tree, watching the passersby. Marta stepped through the front door and slipped in beside him on the stone bench.

Manej smiled at her. "The season is changing, Marta. I can feel it in the breeze, and I can smell it in the air." He gazed up into the sky. "This time of the year, one can smell the grain, ripe for harvest, and the fruit, ripe for picking." He turned to her again. "And how is our young man doing?"

"He's resting quietly," she answered with a nod. She stretched out her legs and smoothed her skirt.

Manej took Marta's hand in his and squeezed. "You saved his life, my wife. He is a very lucky man to have you care for his wounds."

"Well…" She hesitated, catching a wisp of brown wavy hair in her hand and then winding it around the braided bun at the back of her head. "The bones in the palm of his hand and fingers haven't healed straight like I wanted. I don't know if he'll be able to use that right hand very well. I've tried to set the bones as best I could, but I fear it isn't good enough. And the break in his leg? That too, we shall see how well he walks."

Marta and Manej held hands as they continued watching the people pass by.

"He's well on his way to recovering, thanks to you," Manej said.

Something caught Marta's eye. A man had been pacing back and forth across the road. He kept stopping to look in their direction, only to then turn around and pace again.

"Manej, do you know that man over there? He seems agitated and keeps looking over. Oh, there, he's looking at us right now!" Marta lifted her hand to wave at him.

The man across the street conceded and apprehensively made his way through the stream of passersby towards them. He was gaunt, sickly looking, his face drawn and somber. He met their eyes with embarrassed glances.

"Hello, sir. How are you this fine day?" Manej greeted him warmly as he and his wife both rose from the bench. "My wife Marta noticed you across the road. Can we help you with something?"

"Yes," the man said, pursing his thin lips. His eyes shifted nervously. "I've been told you help people when they need food. My family is almost starving. My children have only had one meal a day for so long, and that is very little. My wife and I… we eat a little every day, but now we have run out and… we need… help…"

"Yes, we have provisions. Please come inside," Marta invited. "Is your family nearby? You are all welcome to join us for our evening meal. And we will set you up with more provisions for the next number of weeks."

"My family is just over there, across the road." The man turned to face the roadway and motioned to a woman and children cowering nearby. They all looked so thin.

Marta waved at them and bid them closer. As she watched, the mother picked up the toddler holding onto her skirts and grabbed the hand of the little girl beside her, who in turn held her brother's hand.

Marta waited for a donkey-drawn cart to pass and then crossed the road quickly. She lifted the little girl up into her arms, smiling into the little face that smiled shyly back at her.

"Thank you," breathed the woman, shifting the toddler in her arms. "Thank you so very much."

Marta stroked the little boy's head and laughed when he grabbed her fingers with a boyish giggle.

"This is what we do," she said with endearing eyes. "We help people. This is who we are."

The two women crossed the road with the children and joined their husbands through the front door of the innkeeper's house.

### *Azekah*

Anan was mopping the sweat from his face when he spotted the stranger. The man stood by a stook of wheat that Anan and one of the workers had just cut. The scythe felt heavy in his hands as he twisted gently to stretch the aching muscles in his back.

"Hello," the stranger called out. "I see you're working very hard! How is your crop looking, my friend?"

Anan raised his chin and cocked his head, watching as the man picked his way around the stooks of wheat scattered on the field. He felt annoyed, at first because his father had left him to go running down the road like a school-aged boy, but now because this stranger was disrupting his work. The sun was setting quickly.

"The crop is looking quite good, but I really don't have time to talk with you." Anan frowned. "My workers and I are almost finished for the day."

"Oh, I certainly understand. I'm just wondering if you need some help. What can I do to help?"

Surprised, Anan took note of the man's attire—a clean tunic and cloak. He wore sandals that looked quite different from his own, but they were in pristine shape, like they were newly made.

"Sir, this is heavy labor, especially in this heat." Anan showed the stranger his calloused and blistered hands from working the scythe. "No, I can't ask you to help…"

"Oh, but you're not asking. I'm offering, remember?" The man flashed another smile and pulled off his outer garment, then reached down for the scythe that Anan's father had dropped when he'd suddenly bolted from the field.

"I guess I could pay you," Anan said. "But I've already hired my workers for the season."

"Oh no, my friend! I don't want to be paid. I'm just here to help." Soft lines crinkled at the corners of his kind, hazel-colored eyes.

Anan looked over at the three men in the middle of the field. The workers had stopped to watch. He was perplexed and unsure what to do.

"Well, okay," he decided at last. "I'll go over and help my workers finish up over there, if you'd like to continue here..."

Having made the awkward suggestion, he walked slowly around the standing sheaves. The stranger proceeded to sweep the scythe side to side, slicing through the stalks of grain that fell over in golden waves. He shot a smile at Anan and bent over for another sweep of the blade.

Anan strode to the nearest worker, then glanced back at the man and shook his head in disbelief. It wasn't often that a total stranger offered to work a field in the heat of the day, especially during the harvest when time was crucial. They worked long hours to get the crop in as quickly as they could.

He was still shaking his head when the field's harvest was complete a few hours later. The sun had set and the moon was rising over the hills.

The stranger thanked Anan for his kindness and then went on his way as Anan responded with his own awkward murmur of thanks. He watched the man go, wondering who he was and where he had come from...

## *The Innkeeper's House*

"Please, Aziel, travel carefully," pleaded the innkeeper's wife. "We worry about you! You aren't that strong yet. I wish you would stay a little longer and regain your strength. It's only been a few months."

Aziel smiled at her as he lifted his walking stick. "All I need is this, a bit of food and water, and I'll be fine! Thank you for the loaves of bread, figs, and the wineskin of water!" He reached over to Marta and gave her a warm hug. Then he turned to Manej. "Thank you so very much for your kindness, and the fresh clothes and sandals! I don't know how to repay you. I truly don't. You've helped me so much. How can I ever repay you?"

"I feel the same as my wife," noted Manej. "I wish you would stay a little longer. But I must ask, Aziel, if you would consider going home to your family. Certainly, whatever has come between you and your father can be forgiven. The world is a very dangerous place for a lone traveler. You don't belong here, son. We've done our best to help you heal, but we fear for your safety. Please return to your family…"

Aziel looked down at his feet in shame. "No," he whispered in hesitation. "Going home isn't an option. That village is no longer my home, for I fear my family and my community have disowned me. For me, the road is now my home."

"I'm so very sorry to hear that," Manej said with a deep frown. "Our home is always your home. There will always be a bowl at our table for you, my friend."

Marta and Manej both hugged the young man farewell, then secured his pack of bread, figs, dried fish, and water over and across his back.

As they wished him well, he gripped his walking stick. Aziel shuffled his feet into a steady rhythm, hoping his fellow travelers wouldn't notice the awkward movement that reflected the ache he still felt deep in the bone.

Marta and Manej sat on their favorite bench in the courtyard as the young man ambled away. Manej reached for her hand and squeezed it gently.

"We will pray for Aziel, for protection and guidance," he said as the figure disappeared over the hill. "We've done all we can do. It is now between Jehovah our Lord and Aziel."

It was well past sunset when Marta stood up and spoke to her husband with great heaviness. "I'm going in to prepare our evening meal," she said somberly, her face strained with worry.

She had felt a great burden for their new young friend. He was young and impressionable. He had been near death, and she hoped he would have learned from his experience. She would pray for his protection and guidance, the same as her husband. But she would also pray for wisdom for this impetuous young man. God-breathed wisdom.

Manej caught the gravity in her voice. She was very upset at what had transpired with Aziel, this early departure of the young man who was still healing from the trauma of his attack.

He stood up to follow Marta inside but suddenly heard his name being called from amongst the various travelers on the road. He turned to see a familiar man guiding his donkey briskly towards them in the evening light. The donkey was overladen with bulky sacks.

"Elihu!" Manej called as he rushed over. "It has been so long! How are you, my friend?"

Marta came out of the house at once to give their dear friend a warm embrace. "Elihu, we've just said farewell to Aziel. He is back on the road… but we fear for his safety. We fear for him in many different ways."

"I as well." Elihu turned to Marta and rested a hand on her shoulder, "I will keep an eye out for our young friend while I continue my own journey. Not to worry, Marta." He turned to her husband, beaming "But first I have brought you more supplies!"

Manej and Elihu strode back to the donkey and heaved heavy bags of flour, corn, and beans onto their shoulders. Marta held the door open as the two men carefully unloaded the bags inside. Her heavy heart lifted a little as she watched them work together.

Elihu had brought Aziel to their door, and she was glad to know he wouldn't forget their new young friend. She took one long, last look down the road in the direction of Aziel, hoping to see the figure of the young man peek over the hill.

But no, Aziel was on his journey now. It was up to him to make his way through this world, even though it could be cruel and unkind. She lifted a prayer once again for the young man, and for God-breathed wisdom.

CHAPTER TWELVE

## *The Road*

Aziel had hated to leave the haven of the innkeeper's home. Saying goodbye was difficult, especially with Marta and Manej having been so kind to him over the past number of months, nursing him back to health. He felt guilty that he had no way to repay their kindness, even though they had assured him that everything had been taken care of the night he'd arrived at their home.

He walked along the road, using his walking stick to steady himself. How he'd arrived at their inn was still a mystery. He remembered very little from that night. Snips and snatches of the bandits, falling and tumbling over rocks, hitting the wall of granite at the bottom of the ravine, and then the wolves and a blazing torch… it all seemed like a distant dream that he couldn't quite grasp. The scars on his body proved that it was no dream.

He had been too embarrassed to ask his new friends about the circumstances of how he got to their home, and they hadn't ventured an explanation. It was true that he had put himself in a bad situation and made foolish choices. It felt like he deserved everything he got.

When Manej had pressed him about going home to his family, Aziel hadn't been able to divulge the story. He was too overwhelmed with shame—for demanding his inheritance in a childish tantrum, for forcing his father to sell a portion of his land… land that had been in the family for generations.

Aziel cringed as he remembered his father dipping the family signet ring in wax and then pressing the crest onto the papyrus to transfer the deed to their neighbor. The neighbor had been excited to acquire such choice land. But his father had been very solemn that day, the hurt he endured reflected in his eyes.

"I was too blinded by my own selfishness to see it," he said to himself. "I was just thinking about myself. How I wish I could go back to that day and tell my father to stop. 'Don't sell the land. Don't stamp the deed. Convince me to stay. Warn me of the dangers and temptations that are out here in this world that pull me this way and that!'"

He cringed again. His parents *had* warned him. In fact, they'd had *many* conversations about how the world draws people in, calls them to play on the devil's courtyard and throw caution to the wind.

"We think we're strong enough, but we're not," his mother had said.

Mother… a lump formed in his throat. Aziel felt sick at how he had spoken to his mother. He had been brash with her, so uncaring, so disrespectful. He wished he could take back his words, which had hurt her so deeply. He wished he could apologize to them both for the way he had treated them with insults and accusations.

*And I didn't listen,* he chastised himself. *In fact, I argued with them—told them they were much too set in their ways. I laughed at them and told them they didn't realize the opportunities for ambitious men like me… opportunities that I didn't have in my humble little village.*

At least that's what he had thought. He hadn't even given life in Azekah a chance. He had been too wrapped up in himself, just wanting to have fun. He hadn't wanted to take life so seriously, like his brother.

*I wonder if Anan even misses me. He called me a foolish pup more than once—and I retaliated by calling him an old man before his time.*

"You old man!" Aziel yelled at the vulture staring down at him from a rocky ledge up high on a rock. "Have some fun, Anan! You act like an old man!"

The vulture watched him with interest.

Aziel kicked a stone in front of him. His older brother had been right. He *was* a foolish pup, always looking for the next adventure. But he would never admit that to his brother. Oh no! Anan would be relentless in his reminders of what a self-indulgent fool he had been for squandering his inheritance.

Remorse filled Aziel in waves. He would never give Anan the chance to ridicule him. That's why he could never go back—not to his family, and not to his village. The day he had chosen to publicly shame his family, he had sacrificed his relationship with them. Even the townspeople would have every right to stone him to death for his sinful choices, if they chose to follow centuries of tradition.

"Which is what I deserve," he murmured.

Aziel looked up into the clear blue sky. It was going to be another scorching day.

He kept one foot ahead of the other, trudging along the dusty road. He knew where he was headed: anywhere but the village of Azekah.

## *Kadesh*

Cassia stretched in her bed and slowly opened her eyes. The moonbeam shone through her open window. She could hear the crickets chirping. The early morning was nice and cool, but the day was going to be another hot one!

She quickly changed into her day dress, then swept back the long curtain that hung in her doorway in an attempt to sneak out to the barn. She was eager to see her favorite nanny goat and the twin kids. They were growing so fast.

Stepping out into the shadow, she was startled at what met her. There on a stool in front of her bedroom doorway sat Uncle Balbus, holding a clay cup and smiling at her.

"Good morning, Cassia, my lovely niece," he whispered. "You have finally woken up, my girl. I've been waiting for you."

Cassia could smell the liquor on his breath. Dread choked her. How long had her great-uncle been watching and waiting? She glanced around nervously, not knowing what to do. If she slipped out to the barn now, Uncle Balbus would follow and then she would be caught alone with him, which was dangerous. She knew that in her gut.

She glanced around the kitchen. Where was Bean? He always slept by the door, but he wasn't in sight.

"I locked your rat-of-a-mongrel out in the barn so he wouldn't wake your parents." A sneaky smile crossed Balbus's lips, and he winked at her with those little piggy eyes.

Her stomach churned with disgust. He all but consumed the chair he was sitting on, his rolls of belly folding over his waistband. His round face looked up at her and his jowls shook.

"Come and sit on my lap, little Cassia, just like when you were a little, little girl." He patted his leg. "Come..."

She thought fast. With a quick turn of her heel and a very loud nudge on the wooden door, she marched straight into her parents' room, making as much noise as possible.

"Mother!" she called out. "Did you want me to start setting the table for our morning meal?"

Balbus snorted at the young girl's insubordination, angry that she had thwarted his advances. That was no way to treat her elders, never mind a guest in the house! Her father was going to be none too happy when he woke up from all the noise she was making. Children were not to bother their parents when they were in the bedroom behind a closed door.

He listened smugly to the uproar in the next room and chortled to himself. Yes, she was getting what she deserved.

"Delinquent girl," he snorted in indignation.

"Cassia!" yelled Attilius. "What are you doing in here? You wretched girl... it's too early in the morning. Get out!"

Cloelia gasped. "Attilius, you don't need to speak to our daughter like that. Cassia, I'll come to the kitchen. Yes, yes... but please, daughter, I'll meet you in the kitchen. Go!"

Cassia swept out of the room and walked past the portly man. He caught her by the hand in disgust and held her fast, but she yanked away from his grip with a twist of her arm and strode into the kitchen without a word, shaken and sick to her stomach.

# CHAPTER THIRTEEN

## *Kadesh*

Attilius walked the wheat field, shaking his head. The land was parched and no amount of water carried by hand up from the well seemed to turn the crop around. The wheat had started to emerge, but the kernels were very small. It looked like this growing season would be a disaster.

What was he going to do if there was no crop to speak of? Everyone was feeling the effects of the drought, not just him. The spring rains had come and gone overnight, and then nothing. No rain for months. The ground was cracked with deep fissures and every footstep raised a cloud of dust.

He bent down and scooped up a handful of dirt, letting it sift between his fingers. It turned into fine dust.

Uncle Balbus was waiting for him at the edge of the field. The older gent had been ill- tempered at the breakfast table that morning. He must not have slept very well, especially after all the wine he'd drunk the night before. In fact, Attilius hadn't realized that the man was such a heavy drinker. It was a good thing he often brought his own wine for them to enjoy, as he frequented their home more often now.

"Crop's not looking so good," Balbus shouted. "Do you think you can salvage any of it?"

Attilius shook his head. "By now the grain is ready for harvest. The heat and dry conditions forced the grain to mature sooner than expected. No, I'd say the crop is an utter failure. Even if we did get the rains, it's too late."

He hooked his hands on his hips and shook his head again.

"I don't need to hire any workers either. For the little there is here, I can do it myself, at least with Cloelia and Cassia's help."

They didn't have much money to pay hired workers anyway. They would do it themselves. Still, he was ashamed to share the fact that he had such little funds.

"I'd help you if I could, my boy, but you know my knees don't take to hard labor anymore." Balbus chuckled as he rubbed his bloated belly. "But I can help keep your girls on task if you need someone to supervise!"

Attilius didn't laugh. There wasn't much to joke about this morning. What a terrible start to a terrible day. Cassia, that silly, impulsive girl, had gotten the whole household up and rolling well before sunrise. And now he was realizing that the entire year's crop was a loss. To get to the next growing season, a year away, he'd have to start culling the sheep. And the pasture was as bone dry as the fields. There wasn't much left for the animals to eat, only whatever was left of the previous year's hay.

The sheep and cattle beat their hooves on the dirt, trying to dredge up anything worthy to digest. He could keep the pigs. They'd eat anything and everything, including their own dung. In fact, he'd been feeding the sickly sheep to the pigs over the past month, just to clean up the carcasses. The pigs could tear a sheep limb from limb within an hour. Ugly beasts, they were, but efficient! Their meat was tasty, too, and their fat could be used in many ways. Considering their large litter of piglets, they were a good animal to have around in times of famine.

Attilius pondered the field again. The sight was heartbreaking. His whole identity as a farmer was wrapped up in his land, his crops, and his herds. He was a wealthy landowner and his sheep were known to be the healthiest and strongest in the region. But this relentless drought had outmaneuvered him no matter what he tried.

He could carry buckets of water from the well, but it wouldn't change the outcome, only prolong it. He was defeated.

CHAPTER FOURTEEN

## *Kadesh*

Aziel walked casually through the market square, one hand gripped on his walking stick and the other cradling a sack that held the few belongings he owned. Kadesh was a good-sized town, and the market bustled with activity that morning. He had never travelled this far north of the Sea of Galilee and hadn't known what to expect.

Chickens in wooden cages were stacked at one booth, and sheep and goats were tied to a stake at another. His eyes glanced over baskets of both fresh and dried fish and clay pots full of dried beans. Large pottery jars were filled with wheat and barley, wine and olive oil, and smaller jars were filled with nuts and legumes. Baskets of melons, garlic, leek, and onions dotted the various stalls.

Two days ago, he had eaten the last of the food Manej and his wife had given him. His stomach ached for more and his body felt weak from the strenuous walk.

The odor of barn animals mixed with the smells of fish, fruits, and olive oil turned his empty stomach. The putrid mixture made him feel queasy and he thought he might hurl.

A tall, middle-aged man was selling eggs at one of the stations, as well as two young goats. The kids bleated woefully and jumped at the sudden squawking of nearby chickens. The noise set off the whole flock, producing a deafening cacophony. The young goats scrambled and pulled at the rope around their necks, trying to get away.

The chickens squawked again, bustling their wings and shrieking, disturbing the flocks around them. With one motion, the young goat with brown patches twisted its head and slipped out of its rope and bolted towards Aziel.

Aziel was quick and dropped to one knee, releasing the grip on his walking stick to catch the young kid in his arms. It struggled and strained, but he held it tight to himself.

The owner ran over to him and gathered the kid up and out of Aziel's grip, mumbling a brief thank you before carrying it back to the stake.

Aziel followed him. "Here, I'll hold him while you tighten that rope!" he offered.

The man mumbled his thanks again as the two worked to secure the frightened kid back beside its brother.

"Sir, I see you are a farmer," Aziel said. "Are you hiring any workers for the fall harvest?"

"No," the man muttered. "I don't need any help."

"Do you have a neighbor who needs help with his harvest...?"

Irritated, the farmer interrupted him. "The famine has left me and everyone else in this area without a crop."

"Perhaps you need help with your animals... your chickens or your goats. Do you have sheep that need shearing? Or cattle that need tending?"

"I have no work for you," the farmer spat impatiently.

With that, the man turned to address a customer wanting to purchase some eggs. The day had been difficult right from the start, and now this pest of a boy! He and Cloelia had argued over bringing all their goats to market, Cassia becoming very upset at having her baby goats taken away. He hated himself for doing it, but they needed the money. He had no choice.

Eventually Attilius had agreed that she could at least keep Sunset, her nanny goat, if Cassia would help scrounge for food for the goat, to keep the milk supply strong. She would have to help with the milking of the nanny goat as well... well, at least they had milk.

Aziel knelt near the two young goats that were still pulling at the rope around their necks. He soothed them with gentle hands and stroked their soft necks. He smiled. They were pretty cute, but they were definitely distraught.

"Have you weaned the kids just today?" asked Aziel with a furrowed brow once the customer had gone. "They're about two months old. It's like they're looking for their mother." He glanced up at the farmer. "If they're weaned too early, they could easily get sick."

"I know that!" shot out Attilius, getting even angrier at the presumptuous boy.

He glanced down at Aziel's disfigured hand, then looked into the young man's face and sneered. Attilius then turned again to serve another customer.

Aziel caught the man's look of disgust at the sight of his twisted hand. He brought it down to his side, hiding it from view.

Once Attilius thanked his patron for the coins, he glanced back at the boy and the two kids, still bleating woefully. He just wished the boy would go away. He didn't need to be reminded of how he had pulled the two kids away from their mother. Oh how the animals had cried... and his daughter had cried as well as he literally dragged the young goats down the path away from the barn...

Mostly Attilius was disgusted with himself. Sheep and cattle gave him prestige in the eyes of his community. Now he was reduced to nothing but pigs. He angrily shoved the empty egg baskets into a pile, as the last of the eggs had now sold.

His brooding over the dwindling of his livestock was interrupted by a neighboring farmer who approached him about the kids, offering a decent price.

Purposely, with some force, Attilius nudged the young man who remained crouched beside the kids. He untied the goats from the wooden stake stuck in the ground and handed the rope over to the new owner, ignoring the young man sprawled on the ground.

With the coins in hand and a quick thanks, Attilius packed up his items and proceeded to walk away, leaving behind the annoying young man with the twisted hand.

"Sir, please wait!" Aziel called. He stood up awkwardly and scooped up his walking stick. "I can be of great help to you on your farm. You don't have to pay me. Just one meal a day is all I ask."

The young man continued to plead, jogging up beside Attilius and relying on his walking stick to keep pace.

"I told you I don't need any help," growled Attilius. "I already have someone tending my stock, and I don't need any more mouths to feed. Go away!"

"Just give me a chance. You'll see. I won't be a bother. I promise you! I'll only be a help."

Attilius continued on his way, trying to ignore him, but the young man was persistent and followed him all the way back to the farm. He grumbled to himself as he quickened his strides in an attempt to increase the gap between them. But the young man was determined and no longer even bothered to hide his cumbersome limp.

When they got to the house, Balbus was sitting outside on a bench. "Attilius, my nephew! Come and share a drink with me. I brought an extra bottle for us this evening." The older man squinted at Aziel shrewdly. "And what is this you dragged home from the market?"

"I didn't drag him. He followed me." Attilius scowled, then turned to Aziel. "Okay! If you're so determined to work for me, then follow the path down behind the barn to where the pigs are fenced in. Keep the wolves away. They're hungry too! Halal is down there, but he's useless. Just keep my pigs alive."

Aziel thanked him profusely and lumbered down the path with a new skip in his step. He had a job, even if it was with pigs! Pigs were filthy animals, always grabbing and screaming and biting each other. When they had the taste of blood in their mouths, they were vicious.

Aziel knew his father would be ashamed of him—to ask for work, food and shelter from a stranger was humiliating enough, but to tend a herd of pigs! There were good reasons that Jehovah had forbidden the Israelites from eating pork. Pigs ate the feces of animals and humans. Aziel had seen many houses in this pagan land built with a small upper story room that jutted out over the back courtyard. Pigs were kept underneath to eat the human excrement that dropped to the ground. Pigs also carried parasites and tapeworms that could be transferred to people until they were sick and bloated, eventually dying from starvation.

Yes, pigs were repulsive, but Aziel was hungry and would gladly sacrifice his own self-respect for food.

When the household finished their evening meal, he would go back to the house to retrieve the slop pail for the pigs. Then he would ask for his *own* meal, perhaps bread and a bowl of beans.

He picked up his pace along the path, excited to soon have some food in his belly.

### Azekah

Anan carried the clay jars from the well to the barn and poured the first jar of cool water into the stone trough. He then forked the dried hay into the calf's pen and poured a half container of oats into a second stone trough.

Leaning against a pole, he mopped the sweat from his face with his sleeve. The calf was strong and healthy, its brown coat a glossy sheen. It eagerly delved into the oats and munched enthusiastically, lifting its head to look at Anan with bright brown eyes. It was very pleased with its afternoon meal.

"Ah yes, the fattened calf!" said Anan to the young animal, as if it could understand him. "You get all the attention, don't you?"

While most cattle grazed in the fields, the fatted calf was fed choice grain in a stall and given extra food. Without being able to roam freely and romp with the other calves, it gained weight consistently. Its purpose was an ancient practice and very important in the community; for many generations, the fattened calf was sacrificed and eaten for a variety of reasons—to solemnize covenants, formalize resolutions over water rights disputes, and forge reconciliation between opposing parties.

In their society, most meals consisted of bread, beans, vegetables, olives, fruit and fish, but not much other meat. Meat was an expensive delicacy, especially the meat of the fattened calf.

And whenever there was a public celebration in their land, it was customary to begin with a sacrifice. The meat of the fattened calf was used in the feast. However, the richest and most excellent part of the animal was its fat. As the fat belonged to the Lord, so then it was burned on the altar to the Lord.

Anan smiled at the calf as it lazily chomped its mouthful of oats and wiggled its ears. He poured the second bucket of water into the trough, reached out to scratch behind one of its ears, and laughed.

He lifted his head as his nostrils caught the wonderful scent of stew cooking on the earthenware stand. He made his way outside to see his mother cutting wedges of onions and garlic into the clay pot, placed on the horseshoe-shaped stand against the house. Tomas was with her, helping to clean the dirt off the vegetables he had just dug up from the garden. He glanced up at Anan as the young man approached. The embers under the pot glowed bright orange, with licks of tiny blue flames leaping between the embers. Mother used her outdoor kitchen during the hot summer months.

She glanced up at her eldest son as he walked from the barn. "Anan, there you are! I was wondering where you had disappeared to."

"I was just giving the calf his afternoon meal of oats. Here, Tomas, the calf will need another bucket of water before it beds down for the night." He passed the bucket to their servant.

Tomas nodded respectfully and turned towards the barn.

Anan picked up the large ladle from a small stone table beside her and began to stir the stew. "He's gaining weight quite nicely! And what delicious dish are you making today for your hungry men?"

He bent down to sip a spoonful of liquid from the pot.

"Your father's favorite," she chimed. "Barley and carrot stew with fresh hyssop and sumac spice, and with lots of onion and garlic. Just the way he likes it!"

"Don't forget the celery." He bent down to pick up the freshly pulled celery stalk from the table. "Father likes his celery!"

"Yes, he does, but your brother hates celery, so I'm not sure I should…"

She stopped abruptly, standing up straight to face Anan. Her breath caught in her throat at her lapse in memory. Anan's face fell at the mention of his brother.

"Anan, I'm so sorry."

"Yes, my brother," said Anan with contempt. "I don't think Aziel would mind if you put celery in father's stew."

He handed her the ladle and turned to walk away, but his mother grabbed his arm.

"Anan, wait!" she cried, holding him back. "Please, I'm so sorry! I know this has been hard for you. Please, my son, talk to me."

She reached out for her son's hand, and he turned to face her, his jaw set. She reached for his second hand and held them in her own.

"Anan, you must find it your heart to forgive your brother." She spoke quietly but with intent. "I see the bitterness in your heart, and it's eating you up."

Anan looked deep into his mother's eyes and shook his head slowly. "I'm sorry, Mother, but I can't." He stared down at her tiny hands in his. "How can I? Look at how he's hurt you and Father. Look at how he's broken up our estate through his own selfish desires. Do you not see how he has made our family a joke in the eyes of our neighbors?"

"But you must forgive him," she implored. "I can't lose you too… to the anger that's consuming you. My beautiful son, your life is ahead of you, but this anger deep inside is going to destroy you."

"Mother, do you forgive him? Do you? After all that he's done?"

"Yes, I do, Anan. I do. However, sometimes I have to forgive him multiple times in a day." The glint in his eye caught hers. "I choose to forgive. I choose to forgive your brother, even if it is many times a day, and so must you, my son, to free yourself from the burden of carrying this grudge… this grudge that will grow into hatred. Hatred always brings destruction."

Anan spied her from under heavy lashes, his head bent. He brought her hands up to his lips and kissed them, then turned away sadly. "I can't…"

CHAPTER FIFTEEN

## *The Pig's Field*

When Aziel reached the field of pigs, he immediately saw the man Attilius had told him about. Halal was middle-aged and had scraggly brown hair tinged with grey, including a matted beard and mustache. He was dumping a clay pot of water into the stone trough that stood inside the wooden fence so the pigs could drink without escaping their paddock. They were climbing over each other with shrieking squeals, as if desperate for any kind of moisture.

Halal turned to face Aziel and shot him a skeptical glance. "I see we have another hired man... I suppose the master sees the need of having two of us to take care of these vile animals." He spat at the pigs.

"I'm Aziel," the young man called over the squeals. "How can I help?"

Halal reached for the second container of water. "I don't know how much help you're going to be with that twisted paw of yours," he answered dryly, nodding at Aziel's right hand.

Aziel felt his face flush as he dropped his hand, hiding the disfigurement in the folds of his tunic.

"No matter." Halal shrugged. "I've got one bad leg. Between the two of us, we'll get the work done."

The older man poured the second large clay jar into the water trough, then wiped his hands on his tunic, soiled from years of working with livestock. He knew he reeked of pig manure, cattle dung, and sheep, but he didn't care. He was quite used to the stench of his own body after all the years of hard labor for Attilius.

The two of them worked at bringing the water up from the well. Halal hadn't seen Aziel's limp and the young man was determined to hide the affliction of his smaller, weaker leg as much as possible.

There must have been about two hundred pigs of all sizes, from the newborn weanlings to the massive sows. The boar was the biggest and ugliest of them all. Aziel knew to stay away from that one. He understood why the pagan god Baal was associated with the wild boar; they were grotesque and deadly!

Aziel remembered his father's deep distaste for hogs. Gamaliel loathed the very sight of them and would be horrified at the sight of his youngest son begging to work with them. But the gnawing ache in his belly reminded him why he was there. For now, he just needed some food. After a few days, he would be on his way to the next town to find something better, something worthier of his talents. This was only a stepping stone to better days ahead.

Hahal plopped down under a huge oak tree and leaned against its trunk, stretching out a leg and deeply rubbing both sides of his knee. "Where're you from, Aziel? Your speech tells me you're from further south… I recognize your accent."

"I'm from a village on the other side of the Valley of Elah." Aziel picked up a stick and peeled the bark off it with his good hand. "I doubt you've heard of it."

Halal watched him closely, then took a swig of water from the pot beside him and handed it to Aziel. The water was soothing to the young man's parched throat.

Halal gazed over the land towards the distant hills. "I came from that area myself... but that was a very long time ago," he said slowly. "A very long time ago."

The two men sat in silence, Halal deep in thought and Aziel watching the pigs. Aziel didn't want to share where he came from, or any part of his story. He was far too ashamed and didn't trust this stranger. He needed a friend, not someone to reprimand him for his mistakes.

His stomach growled, reminding him once again of how hungry he was.

"I'll go up to the house to collect the slop pail for the pigs," Aziel said. "You rest that leg of yours."

He got up slowly, again trying to hide how awkwardly he moved. He grabbed his walking stick and made his way along the path to the house.

Aziel heard boisterous laughter as he neared the house constructed from field stones. When he rounded the barn, he spotted his master sitting on the same bench with the portly man who'd been out front when they arrived. Both had been drinking heavily; both were inebriated.

"Sir, I've come for the slop pail from your evening meal," said Aziel. "And might I have my own evening meal, sir?"

"Cloelia!" Attilius yelled, eyeing the young man with a wry smile. "The boy has come for the slop pail!"

The master's wife stepped outside the doors, carrying the clay pot filled with the meal scraps of the day. She thanked Aziel and turned to go back inside. Before leaving, she cast a dirty look at the two men watching her from their perch on the stone bench beside the door.

"Attilius, I tell you, if you weren't my nephew I'd steal your wife away right from under your nose—and keep her for myself!"

cheered Balbus, slapping Attilius on the back as he watched Cloelia step inside the door out of view.

"And some days I'd be grateful if you'd take her off my hands, uncle!" he cheered back.

The two men howled with drunken laughter.

Aziel stood watching them, holding the container against his chest in one hand, the walking stick in the other. "Sir, again, might I ask for my own evening meal, as payment for my service?"

"Payment?" Attilius looked astounded, then burst out laughing while nudging his uncle. "He wants payment, he says! Why, I pay you each time my wife gives you the slop off our table. You're free to pick out the tastiest, juiciest morsel you can find before you dump it into the pig pen."

Balbus slapped his thigh and howled again.

"A pompous young pup picking through the slop before serving it to my pigs—it doesn't get any better than that." Attilius smiled mockingly at Aziel. "The gods have smiled on you. Be grateful I allowed you to tend my pigs instead of throwing you into the pen for pig fodder! Now get out of my sight."

Aziel turned and hobbled back down the path, humiliated. The laughter faded as he walked behind the barn. He looked at the slop pail that reeked of sour fish, now crawling with bugs from standing in the warm kitchen all day.

When he was out of sight, he picked through the scraps in search of anything to eat. All he could find was the rotting end of a cucumber, half a rotting onion, and a bug-infested heel of bread covered in fish guts.

He ate the little he could stomach before continuing down the path to Halal, who was still sitting on the ground against the tree watching the pigs.

"Just pour it in that trough over there," Halal called out. "Then fill those jugs with the husks from that pile. Don't stop until I tell you…"

He pointed to two large clay pots near the pile of dried carob pods that took two hands to carry. Grabbing one of the containers, Aziel made his way to the pile of husks.

He scooped the long, bean-shaped pods into the container, then heaved it onto his shoulder and carried it back to the hogs. Only someone who was desperately hungry would eat the carob pods, but it didn't matter. He longed to bite into the course meat of the skin, knowing they would provide some nutrition, even if they were almost impossible to chew and extremely difficult to digest.

With all his strength, he dumped the full container into the second stone trough, though most of it fell on the ground beside it. Grabbing handfuls, he threw them into the trough but stopped when he had the last one in his hand. Temptation pulled at him. Aziel knew he had reached that threshold of desperation, and he lifted the pod to his mouth, for even just a taste.

Halal stopped him with a shout. "No, no! That's not for you. That's for the pigs—and if the master saw you eating the pig's food, you would be whipped. Trust me, the master cares more about those beasts than he does about you. Get used to the food in the slop pot, because that's all you'll see."

Aziel realized his predicament; these swine were of some value when fattened for the market, but he, a mere worker, had no value at all.

With heavy feet, he continued carrying the huge jars of carob pods to the paddock, dumping them over the fence. The greedy hogs screamed as they clambered over each other, determined to fill their hungry mouths.

Halal settled down under the carob tree, watching Aziel toil in the hot afternoon sun. He felt a bit guilty for yelling at the boy. He was only hungry, and the master wouldn't have seen the boy eat one pod, to be sure. But he himself had learned this lesson when he'd disobeyed the master a long time ago. He had a broken hip to show for it. It hadn't healed properly and arthritis had set in a few years past.

Before the drought, there had been plenty of food and plenty of table scraps, including leftover stews and soups, and all the bread one could eat. But when the rain stopped, the leftovers the family shared with their hired worker had dwindled as well, until there was nothing left to share. Attilius made it very clear that the pigs came first. He had told Halal that he was welcome to leave anytime he wanted to search for better conditions, but Halal knew everyone was in the same desperate state beyond the farm's borders, and he was crippled with that bad hip.

He shifted his weight to sit more comfortably, still watching the young man trudge back and forth from the carob pod pile to the pig's field. The more tired the boy got, the more obvious his limp became. There was no hiding the smaller leg; the left calf muscle was almost half the size of the other. Halal wondered what had happened.

The two were more alike than he had first thought.

He grunted smugly and reached inside his cloak for what was hidden in the folds. When Halal was sure the young runt wasn't watching, he pulled out one of the heels of bread the master's wife had given him that morning when her husband was at the market. She had given him two, both the front and the back slice of yesterday's loaf, unbeknownst to her husband. Cloelia was a compassionate woman and had slipped bread scraps to Halal numerous times during this famine.

Secretly he lifted the bread to his mouth, concealed behind his cloak. He took a bite, all the while eyeing the young man walking back and forth in front of him. He shook his head as if answering the question of whether he would share his bread with this stranger.

"No, he's on his own," Halal murmured with a determined stare, slowly chewing the day-old bread. "There isn't enough for the two of us..."

When Halal finally told him he could stop, Aziel stood and watched the pigs in the evening light. His first day of farmwork hadn't been what he expected. In fact, it had been far from what he'd hoped for.

Discouraged, Aziel sat down beside the older man, leaning against the tree. By now the harvest moon glowed a brilliant orange. He drew his knees up to his chest, pulled his cloak around himself, and stared at the moon, listening to the chorus of insects singing their evening song. He wondered if his family was watching this same orange ball in the sky, and if they were thinking about him as he thought about his home village on the other side of the Valley of Elah.

### *Kadesh*

Cassia lay quietly in her bed, listening to the bellowing laughter outside. Her father and Uncle Balbus were drinking late into the night again, and when they consumed that much wine the two men believed the portly man's stories of tricks and cons were hilarious. Uncle Balbus took great delight in sharing with his nephew his trickery and fraud.

The girl hated hearing and seeing her father drunk like this. It seemed that he had changed from being a gentle, loving father to being more and more like his scoundrel uncle. She loathed the way Uncle Balbus looked at her and made her feel, and he was always at their house now. When he drank too much to walk home, he slept on a mat in the kitchen. Mother wasn't pleased with this arrangement, but Father didn't seem to mind. In fact,

Father enjoyed the camaraderie, as if it was a distraction from these troubling times.

Cassia rolled over and tried to find a comfortable position. It was late at night and the two men's raucous laughter made it impossible to sleep. And it had been a very sad day. Heartbreaking, actually. Her father had taken her nanny goat's babies to the market and sold them. She had begged him to let them stay, but he'd insisted that they needed to go.

So many thoughts tumbled through her mind as she remembered that morning. Her father had been very angry and told her to stop acting like a child, to grow up. She had just stood and watched him tie the rope around the two kids' necks and lead them away. They'd kept looking back to the barn, to her, and calling for their mama while pulling on the ropes around their necks.

A deep sadness overshadowed her, not just about losing the baby goats, but more so about seeing her father act so coldly towards her. Even Cassia's mother's attempts to appease her husband had failed.

Sunrise had called for her kids the rest of the day, looking agitated and trying to climb out of her pen. It broke Cassia's heart to watch the mother long for her babies.

The sudden quiet interrupted the girl's thoughts. The laughter had stopped. The two men had settled down for the night. She only heard the gentle purr of snoring. Good! Now she could finally go to sleep as well. She settled in under her blanket and relaxed.

Wait... what was that? A very faint sound caught her attention—the sound of her doorway curtain moving. Was that a breeze? She held her breath, listening intently.

A footstep near her bed scuffed the stone floor, and then a body crashed onto the bed. Cassia stifled a scream, trying to keep quiet, to pretend she was sleeping. The stench of Uncle Balbus filled her nostrils, a mixture of body odor and wine. He was breathing heavily.

"Hello, Cassia… are you sleeping?" he whispered thickly, his breath hot on the back of her neck. She didn't move, didn't breathe, didn't dare answer. He placed a hand on her shoulder. "Cassia…"

The young girl jerked at his touch—and now he knew she was awake. He chuckled to himself as he squeezed her shoulder.

"Get out of this room," a voice demanded from the doorway. "Get out, Balbus!"

It was Cloelia, raising her voice as she strode over to the bed. "Get up and get out of this room, now!" she threatened.

Balbus caught the glint of the knife in Cloelia's hand, raised high above his thick belly, ready to strike. After a moment, she lowered it and pressed it into his ribs.

He paused, weighing his options, then slowly raised himself off the bed with a snort, doing his best to avoid the threatening blade. He swayed in front of her and took a step past, then stopped and hissed, "Don't you ever speak to me like that again. Or I'll have you stoned, woman!"

Balbus threw open the doorway curtain and staggered out of the room and through the kitchen door to collapse outside on the stone bench.

Cloelia gently laid the knife on the floor and sat on the side of the bed.

Cassia turned to her mother and buried her head in her mother's lap, bursting into heaving sobs. Her mother held her tightly and wept with her, stroking her hair.

"I'm so sorry, Cassia… I'm so sorry… You're safe now… you're safe…"

Outside, Balbus gazed at the orange moon. He stroked the hairs on his chest while listening to the commotion in the girl's bedroom. His failed attempt had only whetted his appetite for the girl. He smiled to himself. He would enjoy this challenge. And if the gods smiled on him, he would have the two of them, Cassia and her mother.

## *The Pig's Field*

The crickets chirped a symphony of song as the stars shone brightly in the Middle Eastern sky. Aziel and Halal had just completed their walk around the swine pen, carrying torches to ward off any wolves that might be contemplating a baby pig for a quick meal. Their task was also to check for any breach in the fence where the swine could make their escape.

They neared the fire between their favorite carob tree and the pig pen. The men propped the two blazing torches into makeshift holders and Aziel sat, leaning against the tree. He wrapped his cloak around his shoulders and curled up, watching Halal stoke the embers. He was hungry and felt weak. The past few months working for his master had proved to be discouraging. There was no escape from the ache in his belly, gnawing at his very senses. The meager scraps of rotting vegetables and leftover beans weren't enough to sustain him. Finding a tiny morsel of meat that still clung to a fish bone was a valuable find.

Shifting his weight, he folded his arms in front of his chest and tried to stop shivering. He didn't know how much longer he would last, for he knew he was slowly starving to death.

Resting his head against the tree, he allowed himself to remember what life had been like just one year ago. As the crickets sang their song, he remembered with a smile how his mother had hated the crickets in the house. She would hear their scritching sound and madly search every corner of the house to find the offender. Then, with great vigor, she would sweep it out of the house with a huff.

He chuckled to himself, thinking about how she would dance with him in the kitchen. And ever since he'd been a little scrap of a boy, she'd carry him in her arms. Even when he was a young man, accidentally stepping on his toes with profuse apologies, they'd laugh together. It felt like just last week.

But "last week" was now months and months ago.

"Where are you from?" Aziel asked the older man quietly.

Halal glanced at his way. "Me? Far from here... I worked with my father, farming the land." He shook his head in self-loathing and spat on the ground. "Not feeding pigs."

"I have so many regrets," Aziel said wistfully. "Halal, do you have regrets when you look back at your life?"

An uncomfortable silence held the air as Halal digested the question. "Yes... yes, I wish I would have appreciated those who truly loved me. My family, my friends, the lovely girl who lived just down the road from my home... I wish I had listened to my father, who warned me about the dangers in the world, and how pride clouds one's ability to make wise choices. I wish I would have listened to my parents more and talked less."

Halal stared into the fire.

"When I was a young man, much your age, my father told me to surrender to the honesty of the moment," he continued. "Look at where you are, what you're doing, and who you're with. If it's good, truly savor that moment, because you'll never experience it again, that set of circumstances. But if it's bad, you have a choice to make, either to continue down the path of certain destruction or change the direction of your steps in hope of a better life." He cleared his throat, the words barely audible. "It takes courage to change the direction of your life, Aziel. But more importantly, it takes wisdom to recognize a path of destruction... and greater wisdom still to know which path to turn towards."

He stoked the fire with his stick.

"I wish I would have listened to my father's words..."

CHAPTER SIXTEEN

## *The Pig's Field*

Halal stood up to add an armful of branches on the fire and stoked the embers again with a long stick. He stared into the flames licking at the thinner slips of wood. The crackling and snapping were somewhat soothing, a familiar sound that reminded him of earlier times when he had tended his father's sheep with the other shepherds. They would sit around the fire at night and share stories of adventure. He smiled to himself as he thought back to his years of innocence and wondering, happiness and sharing with family and community, the joys of being *together*.

He looked over to the young man now sleeping against the tree. He found Aziel to be quite a nice young man, although naïve. The two seemed to get along well, and the younger always let Halal pick through the slop pail first. Halal would play along and pick out the odd fingerful of beans, just so the young man wouldn't get suspicious.

Halal patted his chest fondly, feeling for the heel of bread hidden under his cloak. When the master's wife had slipped him the two chunks of bread that morning, she'd told him there was one for each of them. But what the young pup didn't know wouldn't hurt him.

Well, actually it did hurt him, but Halal shrugged it off. He had told Aziel a long time ago that there wasn't enough work, or food, for the two of them. Why had the master even taken the young boy on, with that left gimpy leg and twisted hand?

He looked at Aziel again and sighed. He was just a teen, not even a man, and his growing body was very malnourished. He was a sorry sight.

At first Halal hadn't liked the thought of having a second worker crowding in on his space, and the little bit of food available, but Aziel had turned out to be a fair worker and helped Halal as much as he could, taking the bulk of the physical labor. Aziel even climbed the carob tree to shake the pods off the branches, as difficult as it was! Before Aziel had come along, the older man had used a long stick to knock the pods down, a tedious chore that was hard on his back and neck. Harvesting the carob pods for the pigs and collecting them into a pile was quite easy now.

Yes, Aziel did his best to help, even though he also struggled. He felt a pang of guilt, however slight, and stoked the fire again.

The two men had become more than mere acquaintances over the past few months. They seemed to have more in common than either wanted to admit. It was as if they each understood the other without the need to share details of their own past… and that was just how Halal wanted it. His own shame, his own interests, his own food, he would keep to himself.

The sound of gentle snoring over by the tree confirmed that Aziel was asleep. Halal reached inside his cloak and pulled out the chunk of bread. The fire snapped and sparked and Halal stared into the fire, getting lost in the changing colors of the flames as they licked the logs in red and orange and azure blue. He bit into the bread again and chewed slowly, savoring it.

He imagined standing in their family kitchen and enjoying the tantalizing smell of boiling vegetable soup and listening to the lilting sound of his mother's voice while she sang. His little sisters tried their best to sing along. He smiled to himself at the warm memories.

His thoughts brought him to a time when he'd been young, like Aziel. When he'd been excited about life and exploring the world, relishing every new experience. He had wanted to see what was beyond the Valley of Elah.

But the life of an adventurer wasn't easy. In fact, he had been shocked at what he saw, having been raised in a good home with loving parents and two sisters in a close community where every neighbor was your friend.

Halal felt the heat of shame rise within him as he remembered what had happened when he'd tried to return. The townspeople had carried out the kezazah ceremony, which took place when an Israelite man left to live among Gentiles only to return with nothing but the clothes on his back and the humiliation of defeat.

He had entered the gates expecting to walk straight down that path to his house to greet his parents with an apology, to be embraced and welcomed home! He had been so naïve.

As soon as he'd entered those gates, the people had crowded around him, aghast at the boldness of his return. The elders had stood before him, one of them holding tight to a clay pot. The men interrogated him with questions he couldn't answer.

He remembered desperately looking for his father through the crowd, but he hadn't been there. According to tradition, his father had to be removed from the ceremony and to stay in his home. Halal was forced to defend his actions to the community leaders alone.

His mother had run through the crowd towards the elders, sobbing and begging for mercy on her son's behalf, but to no avail. They scoffed and turned their backs on her and her defiled son. Halal had brought humiliation and shame not only on himself but also his family. Once again.

"Oh, brothers of the House of Israel, give ear," an elder had cried out. "Our brother, Halal, has left his family and this community to live a life of debauchery and disobedience to our ways, and we are afraid lest his defiled seed mingle with our seed." The man had lifted the pot above his head. "Come and take yourselves a sign for the generations which are to come that his seed mingle not with ours!"

Halal had watched with horror as the elder threw down the large clay pot in front of him, symbolizing the broken relationship that now existed between the community and himself. The elders had judged him for his travels into Gentile lands, labeling him as "worldly." The community wouldn't allow him, or the filth of those people in Gentile lands with their sordid, tainted ways, to ever come back.

He remembered looking down hopelessly at the smashed clay pot that lay in pieces at his feet, and the expression of agony on his mother's face, as the elders turned their backs on them.

Halal had been driven out of Azekah, the town of his birth, never to return. He was separated from his family and community without any hope of restoration.

Stoking the fire again, Halal studied the frail boy curled up at the foot of the carob tree. He didn't know what the young man had done, but surely it wasn't an offence greater than his own. Aziel didn't belong here in this land of harsh ways, cheats and liars, lustful habits and pagan gods. This young man was no match for the devil's courtyard.

He felt a growing sense of compassion for Aziel. He also thought about his own greed over the past few months. He would change. In fact, this time he had tucked the last of the crust back into his cloak. He would share the bread with the boy in the morning—and not just the bread. He would also share his story.

He would speak to Aziel man to man, from one weary traveler to
another.

And he would encourage Aziel to go home. Surely his community would accept him back. Surely the elders in Aziel's village
wouldn't be as judgmental as was his own hometown of Azekah.

# CHAPTER SEVENTEEN

## *Kadesh*

"She lies!" Balbus shouted. "How can you speak such lies, woman? Attilius, that you would take the word of a child, and this... this woman over mine is preposterous."

Cloelia gritted her teeth. "Balbus, I was there. I saw you in Cassia's room, on her bed, and I ordered you out." She hissed at him. "I should have slit your belly open when I had the knife at your ribs."

Balbus fumed, his eyes bulging. "How can you stand here and let her speak to me like that? Be a man, Attilius! She should be stoned for this insubordination." His face flushed with rage as he turned to face Cloelia. "I will have you stoned for these false accusations, woman."

Cloelia persisted. "Listen to me, Attilius. He's had eyes on our daughter since early spring. Heed your wife's words and not this... this wretch of a man."

Exasperated, Attilius raked his fingers through his hair, staring at the floor with crazed eyes. "Stop! Enough! Enough of this. This is ludicrous. Can't you see I have enough to worry about... without these... these outrageous accusations!" He turned to his wife in bewilderment. "Cloelia, you've known Balbus all our married life. You've seen how he has helped us all these years. How dare you accuse him of such things!"

Cloelia caught the smug smirk on his uncle's face.

She gasped at her husband's response. "Attilius, look at him! See how he mocks you. He has brought no good into our home. How can you not see how this man has pursued our daughter? How he looks at her? Look at his face now."

Attilius threw his hands in the air and turned to pace the room.

His uncle's fat lips smiled wickedly. His piggish eyes locked on hers. "I knew you had it in you to be the man of this house, Attilius," Balbus drawled. "Finally! Until now your wife had you whipped. Whipped, I say."

"How dare you?" Cloelia roared at him. "Get out of this house!"

"See how she speaks to us," Balbus blurted. "You should have her stoned for her belligerence. These accusations are without merit!"

"Enough. I said, enough!" Attilius turned and stared down at the portly man standing in front of him. "You are speaking of my wife, uncle. That's enough."

"But she's nothing more than a possession. Your pigs have greater value than this…" He trailed off, searching for words.

Cloelia spun on her heel and walked briskly to the room at the back of the house where Cassia sat on the floor with Bean in her lap. The girl's face was buried in the dog's fur as she wept.

"Get out of my house, Balbus." Attilius stepped closer to his uncle, towering over him. He stared into his eyes and hissed, "Get out!"

## *The Pig's Field*

Startled awake by the sound of screaming, Aziel jumped up in a panic. "Halal! What's happening?"

But the older man wasn't by the fire like usual. Where had he gone?

Aziel grabbed the torch from between the rocks and called out, "Halal!"

The horrific screams were coming from the pig pen, near the water trough.

"Halal!"

Aziel ran as best he could in the dark, carrying the torch. He heard a muffled cry from under the horde of pigs that were screaming and climbing on top of each other. He swept the blazing torch side to side to scare the animals away, kicking them with his feet.

"Halal! Halal!"

There was blood everywhere as the pigs continued their relentless attack. With the taste of fresh blood in their mouths, the stench of open flesh in their nostrils, they craved more.

Aziel kicked at the pigs repeatedly. Dropping the torch, he grabbed Halal's limp body under his arms to drag him out. The older man was covered with mud, manure, and blood, his body gushing red. The pigs clambored over the flaming torch burning their legs, shrieking in pain.

The young man strained to lift him up and over the fence even as the pigs tried to climb him to get to Halal. Aziel held on to the man as tightly as he could. He knew that if he fell, they would both be torn apart by the frenzied pigs. The animals' screams were deafening.

Suddenly, a roar could be heard charging towards them. The massive boar was climbing over the mass to get his taste of fresh meat. Aziel knew he had to act fast, but he had no strength left in his arms to lift the injured man over the fence.

Out of the darkness, a pair of hands reached over and grasped the man's upper torso from Aziel, who then gathered Halal's muddy legs into his arms and swung them over the fence, Aziel following behind.

Together, all three men fell to the ground as the torch sizzled out, the pigs continuing their relentless attack now on each other.

Aziel clutched Halal to his chest, weeping. "What happened, my friend, what happened...?"

"One of the piglets... into the water trough," Halal gasped. "Couldn't get out... tried to help... my head..."

The man began convulsing as blood ran down his face from the deep gash in his forehead; he was going into shock.

Once again, a pair of arms appeared, wrapping themselves around Aziel and his friend, holding them close.

"I'm here with you, Halal," soothed the stranger's voice. "I'm here, my friend."

Halal turned his head in the direction of the voice. His eyes were searching but vacant. "You... you're here... you're here... I know your voice..."

He smiled weakly between gasps, his body shivering uncontrollably.

The stranger rocked the two men in his arms. "Yes, Halal. You are not alone. I'm here, my friend, I'm here."

Aziel bent over the twisted body of his friend and cried, "Oh Halal, please don't die... please... don't leave me, please don't..."

But to his horror, he saw that half of Halal's abdomen had been devoured by the crazed animals that were still screaming in the pig pen.

"Oh, my friend, I don't know what to do..."

Halal groaned as he reached up to touch the young man's cheek. "Aziel..." He struggled to catch his breath. "I'm so sorry, Aziel... I'm so sorry... but please... go home... Aziel... just go home..."

The dying man began to cry and coughed up a mouthful of blood. The fluid oozed on the ground, creating a pool around Aziel and the stranger.

With a final, gasping shudder, Halal's body went limp. His eyes remained open, but without life.

Aziel buried his face into the man's bloody hair as the stranger continued to rock them both in his arms, the young man and his dead friend.

"I'm here with you, Aziel, I'm here," said the stranger. "You're not alone."

# CHAPTER EIGHTEEN

## *The Pig's Field*

The three men scooped dirt onto the grave. No one spoke. Aziel kept to himself, still upset at the horrors of the night before. He was filthy, his clothes, arms, and legs covered in blood, dried mud, and pig dung.

Attilius looked over at the stranger. The man had shown up in the night and helped Aziel retrieve the mutilated body of Halal from the pen before the hogs devoured him completely. According to the two men, Halal had succumbed to his injuries shortly after they pulled him out. Attilius hoped the poor soul hadn't suffered long, but they had no way of knowing how long he had been trampled underfoot. Attilius was sick to his stomach at the horror at what had transpired.

After completing their task in silence, Attilius thanked the stranger for his help. He then went to check the pigs' water trough and walked up the lonely path to the house. By now, mid-morning, there wasn't much left of the pigs that had been trodden under and attacked by their own. He glanced over to Aziel but had no words for the young man. He simply nodded his head and turned away.

Aziel collapsed on the ground near the mound of dirt. Grief and exhaustion overtook him and he began to weep. He violently rubbed his gnarled hand, now calloused and blistered, as if by rubbing harder he could wipe away the memories of the ugliness.

The stranger knelt beside him and squeezed the young man's shoulder in comfort, wiping his own tears with his free hand. The two sat in silence for quite a while.

"Halal was my friend," Aziel eventually said. "And I will truly miss him."

"I know, Aziel, I know."

Aziel shot him a bewildered look. "How do you know my name? You helped me pull Halal out of the pen last night, but where did you come from?"

"I heard your shouts from the road and came at once. I'm so sorry, my friend. I know you and Halal had become friends."

Aziel looked fully into the man's face. The stranger's appearance wasn't at all familiar to him, but he had heard that voice before... a long time ago.

Then he spied the man's sandals. They were strange, but they too were familiar.

And that's when that he realized this was the man who had found him down in the ravine. This was the one who had carried him out of the ditch, away from the wolves. The one who had brought him to the innkeeper's house.

This was the stranger who had saved his life.

"You're the one!" he exclaimed, staring at the stranger incredulously. "You're the one who saved my life."

"Yes, Aziel, I am."

Aziel looked into the man's beautiful brown eyes, but they were so very sad. Tears were running down his cheeks.

"I see the hurt inside you, Aziel," he said kindly. "I call you by name because I know you well." He shook his head slowly, his beautiful eyes glistening with fresh tears. "You don't belong here, Aziel. You belong at your father's side in your father's house. Gamaliel aches for your return."

Aziel was stunned. "How do you know my name? And my father?" he stammered. "Who are you?"

"I am the one who's calling you home. Think of me as your oldest brother, who's come to this cruel and broken land to find you and bring you home."

The young man dropped his head in shame. "I can't go home. I've humiliated my family and they'll reject me. I've embarrassed my father in front of the entire village, and they too will turn me away. I have no home."

"But that's where you're wrong," the man answered. "Your father has been watching for you every day. He sits at the village gates and waits. You will not be turned away by him. He longs for you to come back. You are his son. You will always be his beloved Aziel. So return to your father and let him love you as if you had never left his side."

Aziel was broken; his spirit, his passions, his dreams were all broken. He pondered the notion of going home, back to Azekah on the other side of the valley. Would he be welcomed back, or would he be turned away?

He held his head in his hands. *How many hired servants of my father have bread enough to spare? And here I am dying of hunger.*

Did he dare to believe there was a chance for reconciliation? Was there a glimmer of hope, ever so faint, for him to return home?

"How?" Aziel asked the stranger. "How can I return?"

The man rose to his feet. "You will find a way, Aziel. It takes great courage, but you will find a way."

The young man watched the stranger walk away from the pig pen and up the path that led behind the barn.

*I will get up and go to my father,* Aziel decided. *I will say to him, "Father, I have sinned against heaven and against you and am no longer worthy to be called your son. Make me as one of your hired servants."*

He looked over to the pig pen where the pigs lay in the dirt as if nothing had happened the night before. His eyes fell on the patch of blood on the ground, now a caked stain, and remembered Halal's last words: "Go home…"

Was there any hope left in him? Was there a chance he would be accepted back? Did he have enough courage to try?

## *Kadesh*

Attilius sat at the table, his shoulders hunched in defeat and his arms limp on the table. His wife and daughter had kept themselves at a distance from him ever since the argument with his uncle. For weeks Cassia had been spending more time out in the barn with her animals. It was like her spirit was broken. The girl had changed from a laughing, bubbly young lady to a ghost of a girl. Her young innocent beauty had been replaced by sullenness and she looked at him with contempt. Cloelia continued with her household duties, but she avoided him as much as possible, offering curt answers and somber silence. His heart ached for the loss of their family bond.

He held the mug of wine in his hand and lifted it to his lips, then stopped. He set it down. He had been relying on the drink to carry him through this difficult time. The land was dry and cracked. A hoard of locusts smothered the crops, devouring the last living greenery. The famine had done him in, and he was drowning his sorrows in drunkenness, no thanks to his uncle's influence.

Balbus didn't come for his usual visits anymore. His uncle was not the man Attilius had thought he was. He had caused great division in their home. The uncle had crossed a line and was no longer welcome.

Truthfully, Attilius did believe his wife's account of what his uncle had been up to, but it hurt to know that his own uncle would treat his family this way… would treat *him* this way. Balbus had been like a father to him ever since his own father's tragic death. After the boating accident, Attilius had searched for a father figure to replace the one he lost—not intentionally, but from a deep empty hole in his heart. Uncle Balbus had filled that role.

However, no true and loving father would ever treat him or his family this way. A true and loving father would protect his family.

Attilius felt the heaviness of his guilt. Balbus's behavior towards their daughter was deplorable and now Cassia had been withdrawn for months. He wondered how long his uncle had been after the girl. But Attilius had been too distracted with the operations of the farm, the poor crop, and the loss of livestock to notice.

And then there had always been the drink to dull his senses, to calm his nerves and stop that never-ending barrage of thoughts that reminded him of his failures.

He didn't know how he could ever make things right with her. How could he get back his sweet, happy Cassia? His heart ached for his daughter.

The death of Halal had shaken him to the core. The man had worked for him quite a few years, yet Attilius had never tried getting to know the man. Yes, Halal had been slow with that crippled leg of his, but he'd been a decent man and dedicated to their farm.

Attilius felt another twinge of guilt that he hadn't been kinder. He should have been more patient. More encouraging, rather than crude and insulting. His tragic death in the pig pen had been horrific, only adding to this poor man's life of misery.

And what about Aziel, or the stranger who had come up the road to help? After the stranger's departure, Aziel had come up to the house, well into the afternoon, and shared his plans to leave. He hadn't said where he was going, just that he would be gone by evening.

The guilt deepened as Attilius remembered how cruelly he had treated the young man. The boy had only wanted food, but Attilius had been too caught up in himself and his own discouragement to see the boy as a fellow human, just as desperate as himself.

Before Aziel left, Cloelia had said she would fill the boy's pack with bread, dried fish, and water for his journey.

Attilius pondered Cloelia, his beautiful wife. She was such a wonderful woman, more beautiful on the inside than he could put into words, so generous and kind. She was a good wife and mother and didn't deserve the cruel words of his uncle, or his own cruel words as her husband.

*I didn't defend her,* he thought shamefully. *Instead I accused her of lying.*

His heart ached for his wife and for the bond that was broken between them.

His brooding was interrupted by a gentle knock on the door. At first he ignored the knocking, hoping that the visitor would go away so he could be alone with his thoughts.

The knock sounded again, this time louder.

Frustrated, Attilius stood up and opened the door to see the stranger in front of him, the stranger whom he thought had already left.

"What do you want?" Attilius mumbled wearily. Honestly, he didn't have the energy for whatever this man wanted. "I don't have time for you."

"Just a cup of water please, sir."

Attilius shrugged. "Yes, come in."

He led the man into the kitchen where the clay pot of water stood. He filled a wooden mug and handed it to the stranger, slightly exasperated. The man sat at the table while Attilius resumed his spot on the chair.

He sat back, eyeing the stranger suspiciously. "What are you doing here? How did you come to help my workers last night?"

"I was walking along the road when I heard the pigs' screaming and knew there was trouble. It was good I came when I did, for that young man would not have been able to pull Halal out on his own. He would have gotten himself trampled and attacked." The man hung his head. "It was a horrible way for Halal to die. Swine are vicious when there's blood in the air."

"Look," Attilius said impatiently, rubbing his face with both hands. "I don't know who you are or why you're here, but I don't want to talk to anyone. I want to be by myself, to sort some things out. And I need to find another worker because now *both* of my workers are gone."

"Yes, I know." The stranger nodded. "Aziel has decided to go back to his home village and his father's house."

Attilius frowned. "His father's house? I thought he was an orphan… he was in such a desperate state. Why wouldn't he have gone home long ago?"

"Well, he wanted to live his life his own way, without being watched, or judged, by his father, his family, or his community. He didn't want to be responsible to anyone. He wanted to be free! What he didn't realize is that he had been the freest in his father's house. Even when they argued, Aziel's father still deeply cared for him and wanted that relationship restored. Aziel needs to see that for himself."

Attilius listened intently, looking down at the floor and thinking of his own family. They too argued. The relationships between them were broken.

"Attilius, I see the hurt inside you," said the stranger softly. "Your wife and daughter miss you. You've been gone from them a very long time. Yes, you're here in body, but not in your heart."

The man looked at Attilius intently but with kindness in his eyes. Attilius glanced up and frowned in confusion. This man had the deepest compassion for him and his little family. It was like he knew them. How?

"Attilius, your wife and daughter need you to be the leader in your home, to love them and protect them, to cherish them more than any other friend or family member on earth. Jehovah has handpicked *you* to be their protector and provider as husband and father. They need you now more than ever in this time of trouble, of famine, of boundaries crossed by your uncle, of mistrust and separation between you in a changing culture that is often cruel. My friend, as the leader of your home, it is your responsibility to bring your family together again."

Attilius continued to stare at the floor. He knew what he needed to do to make things right. But it took a lot of courage for a man to be vulnerable with the people he loved. He had been raised to believe that to be seen as a strong man, he dared not show weakness, not to anyone.

*Then again,* he thought wryly, *that was driven into my head as a boy by my uncle. That might just be one more thing Balbus was wrong about.*

# CHAPTER NINETEEN

## *The Road*

Aziel placed one foot in front of the other, walking gingerly on the stony pathway in his bare feet. After a while he stepped off the road and sat on a large boulder to tend to his open wounds. His feet were raw, blistered, and bleeding.

He rubbed his foot as deeply as he dared. He tore the sleeve from his tunic, surprised at how easy it was; the garment was more threadbare than he'd thought. He made two strips from the fabric and used them to carefully wrap each tender foot.

Reaching into his bag, he pulled off a chunk of bread from one of the loaves his master's wife had given him. Cloelia was a nice woman, very kind. He knew they had a daughter, but he didn't see much of her as she spent most of her time with the farm animals in the barn. The girl—really, a young lady in her teens—seemed to live in the shadows. Her father was a tyrant, so Aziel understood why she would stay away from him.

No, the master of the house hadn't been a kind man at all. Attilius had only ever showed compassion when they were digging the grave. Even then, it had seemed more a result of exhaustion than remorse.

Aziel had thought he would receive the brunt of the master's anger and blame for the death of Halal. But no, their employer had quietly gone about preparing the body for burial and shoveling the dirt to close the grave. The men had all worked in silence, each dealing with their own thoughts.

Aziel wished he could have known Halal better, but the man had kept very much to himself and shared nothing of his past. Aziel knew the elder had been a fellow Israelite in a pagan land, but he would never know how he'd ended up in Kadesh, working for Attilius, the wealthy farmer...

The wealthy farmer? For all his arrogance, Attilius had been reduced to a pig farmer. Yes, he had kept his land, but with the severe famine it was impossible to grow a crop.

Aziel shook his head sadly. *Life has a way of humbling us all, each in our own way.*

Memories of the tavern, the music, and the dancer flooded his thoughts. Another wave of shame flushed his face. He knew that the many things that happened to him were direct consequences of his own poor choices.

He brought the goat skin full of water to his dry and parched lips, spilling some of the water down the front of his tunic. He looked at his clothing. He was a mess; his tunic was full of mud and manure and stained with Halal's blood. He reeked of sweat and swine and was appalled by his own state of poverty. He had nothing but the clothes on his back, and barely that.

Perhaps his father wouldn't even recognize him. Perhaps he could offer himself as a worker. At least the workers on his father's farm had food to eat and a roof over their heads. Over time, he could pay his father back with his wages. It would take years, perhaps a lifetime, but it was the only way he could return.

Aziel tucked the bread into his bag, ate a few bites of fish, then reached for his walking stick to resume his journey. His feet were still tender but at least the cloth wrappings offered some protection from the rugged terrain. He trudged on, chewing the fish and digesting his predicament. He had walked away from his family and community by his own accord. Both had the right to turn him away. It was what he deserved. He also knew he could be stoned for his insubordination.

But if he continued down the path in the opposite direction from his father's house, he would soon be dead. It took courage to return to Azekah, knowing he had only a slim chance of being welcomed back.

He would take that chance, though he knew it came from a place of desperation rather than courage.

Aziel practiced his speech as he continued down the road well after dusk. He walked by the light of the moon until he could walk no further, the wrappings on his feet having fallen away some miles ago.

His body shook with exhaustion and he stumbled forward, falling onto the ground. Sharp stones grinded into his knees. On shaking legs, he slowly rose to his feet and made his way to the side of the road towards a large rock.

He lowered himself down against it and once again brought out his pack of food and water. Holding the last of the bread, he began to tear it apart.

He remembered his father's house and the many prayers of thanksgiving they had offered at each meal. His father had always been faithful to lift up praises and thanksgiving to Jehovah. Father would reach out and take his mother's hands in his, then bow his head to pray for their daily sustenance and for the blessings Jehovah had provided their family that day.

Aziel gazed into the night sky, now enveloped in royal blue. His words caught in his throat as he whispered a feeble prayer of thanksgiving.

"Jehovah, my Lord," he stammered. "I don't deserve Your mercy... but hear my prayers, Oh Lord, save me..."

He gasped in sudden awareness, remembering his earlier years in the synagogue with the teachers of instruction in the words of the Torah. It had been mandatory to know the scriptures. He had memorized the words, although he hadn't accepted their meaning into his heart.

Until now.

He lifted his face and recited the words of David from the Psalms, his voice thick. "Save me, Oh God, for the waters have come into my soul. I sink in the deep mud, where there is no way to stand. I have come into the deep waters where the floods flow over me... I am weary of my crying, my throat is dry, and my eyes fail while I wait for You." He groaned aloud, closing his eyes. "Oh God, You know my foolishness. My sins are not hidden from You. Let not the flood water flow over me, nor the deep swallow me up, nor the pit shut its mouth upon me. Hear me, oh Lord, for Your loving kindness is good. I know it is. Turn to me according to the multitude of Your tender mercies. Do not hide Your face from me, for I am in trouble. Come closer to my soul and redeem it. You have known my deplorable state, and my shame and my dishonor. They have broken my heart, and I am full of heaviness."

Hot tears trickled down muddy cheeks.

"I looked for some to take pity, but there was none, and for comforters, but I found none." His voice broke as he gently wept. "But I am poor and sorrowful. Let Your salvation, oh God, set me up on high."

Aziel wiped his face with his hand and repeated the scriptures with determination as if trying to convince himself of their truth.

"I will praise the name of God with a song, and will magnify Him with thanksgiving." He gasped in anguish. When his voice broke again, he lowered his face into his hands. "I am poor and needy. Make haste unto me, oh God. You alone are my help and my deliverer. In You, oh Lord, do I put my trust."

## *The Rocky Ledge*

The vulture spread its charcoal-colored wings from its perch on the rocky crag, a nightly ritual to cool its body from the heat of the day. From its vantage point, it could study the young man huddled against a boulder in a deep, exhausted sleep. The giant bird had been watching him for some miles now, following stealthily behind, circling above unnoticed. The heavy scent of blood and raw flesh hung in the air and the vulture knew this would be an easy meal.

It cocked its head, pondering the situation as it stretched its wings further. Temptation and curiosity beckoned for it to swoop down for a closer look, and maybe steal a quick bite before the man fully awoke.

The bird leaned forward to fall into flight, its talons digging into the rock, when a gentle breeze blew against it, holding it back. The vulture hesitated in confusion. A force greater than itself held the bird in its place on the rocky ledge. It fluffed up the sandy feathers that collared its neck, then settled back against the rock, tucked in its wings, and watched the young man sleep through till morning.

## *The Road*

Aziel woke just as the sun peeked over the hills. After tending to his feet as best he could, he carried his walking stick and continued down the road towards the forest of terebinth trees, heading into the Valley of Elah.

As he walked, he practiced his speech once more. "I will say to my father, 'Father, I have sinned against heaven and against you and am no longer worthy to be called your son. Make me as one of your hired servants, that I might repay you...'"

## *Azekah*

Gamaliel worked together with his servant Tomas to repair the crack in the roof. They were perched high on the roof with a bucket of water, as well as dried clay and a ladle. The dry summer had created a fissure on the roof that was sure to leak when the seasonal rains came.

The older man scooped a handful of dried clay into a bowl and poured some water, just enough to mix well but not too thin to compromise the integrity of the clay. He ladled the mixture onto the crack and spread it evenly. It would be another hot day, perfect for repairing the roof. The clay would bake in the sun well before the fall rains.

Tomas poured more dried clay into his own bowl with a splash of water and mixed it thoroughly. The men worked side by side throughout the morning, hoping to complete their task by high noon. But the sun beat down on them and the coolness of the morning had long passed.

Gamaliel sat back, stretching his aching muscles. "It feels warmer than yesterday, Tomas," he said, wiping the sweat from his face with his sleeve. "We may have to finish this in the evening when it's cooler."

He glanced over at his servant, who looked as exhausted as he felt, even though Tomas was thirty years his junior.

Gamaliel slowly made his way to a standing position, offering his hand to help Tomas to his feet. The older man shook out his legs, which tingled from kneeling too long, and then gazed over the village. The land stretched out before him. His eyes scoured the road as it arced its way out of the clusters of terebinth trees leading out of the valley. The view of the Jerusalem mountains and coastal plain was stunning from this high perch.

A movement far off in the distance caught his attention. He noticed a figure making its way up out of the valley.

He squinted against the sun's brightness, shielding his eyes with his hands. The figure was moving ever so slowly along the winding road, shuffling with an unsteady limp. Gamaliel could make out a gaunt figure clinging to a walking stick with each forced step. He walked along in bare feet.

*That's odd*, Gamaliel mused. *The man is barefoot, and in rags... is this a runaway slave?*

Only when the young man looked up and shielded his own eyes did Gamaliel recognize him.

"Aziel!" he breathed. He turned to his servant. "Aziel has come home! Quick, Tomas, get my best robe—and my ring, and shoes. Quickly!"

Gamaliel rushed to the ladder and climbed down as fast as he could move his cramping legs. Upon reaching the ground, he broke into a sprint, almost tripping over his tunic. He gathered up the skirt of his clothing and ran to the front of the house.

"Aziel is home, Ednah! Our boy has come home!" he shouted as he ran past.

Ednah stared out the window in shock and horror. Her son was coming home, but she knew the elders of Azekah would have the final say. He could be turned away, rejected by the entire village, or even stoned to death. Ednah feared for his life.

But Aziel was home! She rushed out the door, her heart in her throat. Relief mixed with dread as she followed her husband down the path.

Gamaliel was already at the village gates by the time the townspeople realized what was happening. They stood aghast as the older man held up the skirt of his tunic to run faster, showing his bare legs to the gathering crowd. They were horrified to see a man over thirty years old bare his legs in public. This was outrageous!

The elders went for the clay pot, readying themselves for the coming interrogation and kezazah judgement. For over a year they had waited for this day, the giant pot ready to be used should the defiled young man return.

As Aziel neared, his father ran faster to meet him on the other side of the gates, calling to him. "Aziel! Aziel, my son! You've come home!"

Aziel stumbled into his father's arms and fell to his knees.

Gamaliel gathered the frail and weary boy to himself, kissing him on his neck and head. "My son… oh, my son, how I've missed you!"

Aziel started to speak, his voice hoarse. "Father, I have sinned against heaven and against you and am no longer worthy to be called your son…" He forced the words between cracked lips.

But before he could finish, Gamaliel turned to his servant who was running up behind him, his arms full. "Tomas, bring me the robe so I can put it on my son, and the ring on his finger, and sandals on his feet!"

"But Father…" Aziel wept, dropping himself to the ground at his father's feet. "I have sinned against you. I don't deserve this…"

Gamaliel knelt, gathered his son in his arms once again, and held him close. He stroked the mop of hair that matted the young man's head and rocked him gently.

"Oh Aziel, my beautiful boy, I've been waiting for you for so long. So very long. You've come home, my son… I love you so very much! Come, let us go up to our home—*your* home, Aziel. Your home!"

A crowd had gathered behind Ednah at the village gates, scrutinizing the three men in the middle of the road. Their murmurs and mutterings grew louder as they watched Gamaliel break the customs of their people. Gamaliel had forgiven his son and was restoring him to the family, to the community, before the ceremony could take place.

With a sweeping motion, Gamaliel wrapped the silken robe around Aziel's hunched shoulders, covering the clothing that testified to the stench and filth of his sordid life. With his own covering, the father enveloped the son with his robe of acceptance and forgiveness.

He then took Aziel's hand in his and carefully slipped his signet ring on his son's calloused and gnarled finger. He gazed up into his son's weathered face.

Aziel sat motionless on the ground, staring at the ring on his twisted hand and trying to make sense of it all. Perplexed, he looked into his father's face, his wonder met with the father's deep affection. Unconditional love and understanding which words could not express poured into the young man's very soul.

Gamaliel lowered himself to the ground and took Aziel's foot into his hands. He gasped at what he saw: the raw and bloody feet from miles of walking a wilderness road. At once he tore the hem off his own tunic, made them into strips, and gently wrapped his son's feet.

Aziel wiped tears from his sunbaked cheeks. "Father, I... I don't deserve this..."

"Aziel, you are my child. You will always be my child. Always." Gamaliel smiled. His son was almost unrecognizable, yet he would always know this boy of his, his Aziel.

With the rest of the townspeople, Ednah watched from the gates in astonishment. She understood the public statement her husband was making; he was showing unconditional love for the entire community to witness. By giving their son his favorite robe, Gamaliel was covering the boy's shameful past, welcoming Aziel back into the family and restoring the boy's position as his son. By giving him his signet ring, Gamaliel was restoring Aziel's authority to conduct the family business in his father's name. And the new sandals on his feet restored the boy's dignity, as only slaves went barefoot.

Through all these actions, Gamaliel was acknowledging his son's restoration to the family—and he was doing it in front of his entire community.

The men rose from the ground and slowly walked together towards the gates. Gamaliel's arm wrapped around his son, and Tomas held Aziel's arm on the other side, both holding him up as he tenderly approached the village.

Ednah ran up to them, crying. She hugged her son with tears streaming down her face. She kissed Aziel on the cheek as he took his mother into his arms.

Relief and remorse welled up inside him and they sobbed together. He had missed his family more than he had ever realized. He was home, and not rejected and turned away as he had expected but accepted with love and forgiveness.

The townspeople gathered around them, chattering amongst themselves at the strange turn of events and Gamaliel's shameful behavior.

The elders broke through the crowds, one of them holding up the clay pot, ready to throw it down at Aziel's feet. But the old man, Reuel, grabbed the arm of the leader of the elders.

"No!" the old man ordered, his voice shaky. "Let them be! This son has returned. This son has been forgiven."

The elders stared at Reuel in disbelief. They then turned back to Gamaliel and watched as the family walked past, incredulous at what they were witnessing.

Reuel spoke again. "I said, leave them be," he repeated. "The prodigal son has returned."

"Tomas!" Gamaliel shouted to his servant. "Slaughter the fattened calf, for my son has come home." Then he turned to the crowds. "Come! Let us all celebrate this wonderful day. Everyone, come!"

# CHAPTER TWENTY

## *Azekah*

It was dusk when Anan started his walk home from the farthest field on the farm. He had been working the soil along the field's edges to prepare for the winter. Working proactively in the fall made his work easier in the spring, to control the weeds and decrease the amount of soil erosion from strong winds.

He was making his way up an incline to the house when he heard music and laughter from the other side of the hill. As he rounded the top, he saw their house brightly lit with many lanterns and candles. He spotted Tomas lighting a lamp out by the back door.

"What's happening?" he asked the servant. "Why the celebration?"

"Your brother has come home. Your father has killed the fattened calf, having welcomed your brother back home, safe and sound."

Anan stared at the servant, perplexed. Through the open doors and windows, he saw their neighbors dancing to lively music. The family table was adorned with baskets and bowls filled with a variety of food. Fresh fruit and bread and large slabs of cooked meat adorned the many platters.

Fresh meat... the fattened calf...?

He turned to Tomas. "The fattened calf, you said?"

Instantly, the burn of jealousy and anger blazed inside him.

"Come, Anan," bid the servant. "Your brother has returned and the whole community has come to celebrate with your family."

This was outrageous! For his father to be this extravagant at the return of a useless son meant he had clearly lost his mind.

"Absolutely not!" Anan stood with feet firmly planted, watching in outrage at the celebration. This was madness!

The servant rushed into the house to join the festivities, and soon Gamaliel stood in the doorway. He rushed out to greet his oldest son, grasping his arm.

"Anan! Come and celebrate, for your brother has returned."

Anan shook off his father's grip and glared down at him. "Look! All these years I have served you. I've never gone against you or your instruction. Yet you never gave me even a goat that I might celebrate with my friends! But as soon as this son of yours, who has squandered your life's work with prostitutes and wild living... as soon as he returns, you kill the fattened calf for him?"

Gamaliel looked deep into Anan's eyes. "Son, you are always with me, and all that I have is yours. We must come together and celebrate. Your brother was dead to us, and now he is alive again. He was lost and now is found."

Anan shook his head in disbelief, glaring at his father. "How can you accept him into your home? *Our* home? This welp of a boy filled himself with the filth of the world. Why do you welcome him back with open arms, with music and dancing? And the fattened calf! How can this be?"

He turned his back on his father and strode away from the house with determined strides. Gamaliel helplessly watched his oldest walk away, angry and dejected.

## CHAPTER TWENTY-ONE

### *Azekah*

Quick steps and a tempered fury brought Anan to the sheep paddock. He couldn't believe what he'd just witnessed.

He had headed back up the hill when a sudden burst of merriment and laughter came from the house. The celebration had spilled outside and into the courtyard, the musicians continuing their song under the lemon tree as the people danced with joy. Anan had spotted his mother hand in hand with a thin young man with black curly hair. He'd swung her around gently and caught her up in his arms. She'd laughed as she looked up into his face...

It was Aziel.

A roar surged up from deep inside Anan as he turned away and marched to the far side of the yard, approaching the sheep paddock. He had to stay far away from the house. Far away from the music. Far away from his brother.

Anan struck the stone wall with the stick in his hand, breaking it in two. The extravagance of the celebration left him utterly astonished, and the amount of money, *his* money, that it had cost for his father to put on this feast was intolerable... this was a mockery of a year's worth of hard work. His hard work. It was utterly loathsome.

"Disgraceful," he seethed between clenched teeth. "What a useless boy! How dare he come back after all he's done? He's nothing more than a reckless, entitled fool. No one should celebrate his return…"

He paced along the stone fence with long strides, raw rage overtaking him.

"I cannot believe this. The fattened calf—for *him!*"

It was better that he didn't go into the house. For if he had seen his younger brother, he would have killed him.

His hateful eyes glared into the paddock as he placed his workworn hands on the stone wall. He watched the sheep in the paddock, hoping it would calm him. The pulling ache in his chest told him that he needed to rein in his mounting fury. His heart was beating hard; he was even shaking. In this state, he knew something or someone would get hurt if he didn't get ahold of himself.

He dropped his forehead onto his arms and took a deep breath, closing his eyes. His thoughts returned to all the events of the past year, replaying all the times he had watched his father drop everything and run to the road, all the many months his mother had wept silently in the kitchen as she baked and cooked and tended to the garden, all the many months that he himself had needed to work even harder because his younger brother had left.

Throughout the entire last year, *he* had kept the family together. *He* had kept the farm going. *He* had put up with the disgrace in the community.

Angry tears welled up in his eyes. He brushed them away, muttering under his breath.

The pressure in his chest had increased, and he raised his hand to his left side, forcing slow breaths, listening to the sound of his racing heartbeat.

*Slow down,* he said to himself. *Just slow down…*

Anan focused his attention on the breeze that cooled the night air and the insects that chirped all around him. Soon his breathing was normal once again.

Resting his chin on his hands, with somewhat restored peace, he watched an ewe with her twin lambs. She nudged and settled them down for the night. They stayed near their mother, each taking their turn to suckle their evening meal.

*Twins,* he thought.

When he and his brother had been in their early teens, strangers to their village had thought they were twins. Anan hadn't reached his full height of six-four, but Aziel was growing fast. They looked alike, true. They were far from being the same, though. One was serious about life while the other thought life was a toy to be played with.

Truth be told, however, he *was* envious of his younger brother. Aziel was the jokester, the center of his parents' affections. The younger brother was the one everyone loved. Life seemed to be so easy for him, just one big adventure.

Anan felt justified in his rant. Of the two brothers, *he* was the eldest, the one who had remained dutiful to the family and their farm. *He* had remained committed to the family and loyal to their father. He had felt obligated to stay home and work on the land after his brother left.

The situation just wasn't fair. His brother deserved nothing more than a life of servitude in his father's house, not a celebration. The pressure in his chest tugged at him again, and Anan forced himself to listen to the evening sounds…

The sun had now set and the toads joined in on the nightly chorus. He was still deep in thought, brooding, when a voice interrupted the quiet night air.

"Anan, my friend! I see you're not with your family to celebrate your brother's return."

Anan slowly turned. The voice was familiar, but he didn't recognize the figure coming out of the shadows until the man stood directly in front of him. It was the stranger who had helped him and his workers harvest the grain a number of weeks before.

He turned back to face the sheep, scowling at the intrusion. He wanted to be left alone—yes, to brood, to be angry, to be exasperated at his father for foolishly accepting his younger brother back into the family. He was also angry at the elders for not smashing that clay pot right in front of the boy the moment he'd stepped inside the village gates. That was their tradition, to reject a wayward son.

*I would have smashed that pot at his feet,* he thought. *I would have grabbed the first rock myself to begin the death sentence of stoning.*

The stranger came up beside Anan and the two stood in silence as they watched the sheep, some of which were still grazing while others bedded down for the night.

"Your brother has come through a very difficult journey…"

"I don't care!" yelled Anan. "I just don't care. He deserved everything he got. He could have died, for all I care. He should never have returned, and my father should never have accepted him back. And then to celebrate? It's outrageous."

He turned steely eyes to glare at this man. Then he went back to the sheep, turning his back to the stranger.

"Anan, you must remember your father's heart," the man said tenderly. "The same love he has for you, over all these years, he has for your brother. Aziel's choice of a different path doesn't mean your father loves him any less. Yes, Aziel was foolish. Yes, he made mistakes. Many mistakes. But he has come back to your father with remorse. Your father has forgiven him, and you must forgive him as well… or else your anger and bitterness will destroy you. It will eat you up from the inside, like an abscess that grows into poison that tortures you till your last breath."

Anan growled at the man. "Who are you to tell me this? Who are you to know what I think, or what my father feels, or what my brother has been through? You don't know this family. Who are you anyway?"

"Anan, I am like *your* older brother. And I've come to call you back to your father's house." As the man continued, a flicker of understanding flashed in Anan's eyes. "I see the pain inside of you. I know that you're angry and hurt. You too were rejected by your brother, just as your parents were. But now it is *you* who is rejecting them."

A shadow of remorse crossed Anan's eyes as he gazed into the eyes of the stranger standing in front of him. He looked away and stared at the sheep. He shoved that brief feeling of remorse deep inside.

"Do you remember when the sheepherder, Shimon, went out and searched for his missing lamb?" the stranger asked.

Anan made a confused expression. "You were there?"

"He left his entire flock behind and celebrated with the community when he finally found it. Do you remember?"

Anan nodded silently.

"The same is true with your father. He couldn't rest until *both* of his sons were by his side. Your father loves you and has always wanted the best for you—for both you and your brother."

"I have stayed here by my father's side, all these years," Anan spoke through gritted teeth. "I have followed his *every* decision, his *every* instruction, and yet he kills the fattened calf for the son who has disgraced him."

"Anan, you have followed your father's direction, yes. But did you follow because of duty to him, or through a desire to please your father with a servant's heart? Do you truly know your father's heart? Do you not see his love for you?"

Anan felt the compassion in the man's words. "Who are you? You say you're like my own older brother, yet I don't have one."

"I am *like* your older brother because I left my own Father's house to go and find your brother and bring him home," he shared gently. "Now I come to bring *you* home, Anan, to your father. Remember your father's heart. He loves you and only wants to bless you—not to hurt you, not to make you sad or angry, but to be in communion with you. He loves you, more deeply than words can share. He always will."

Anan carefully studied the man's face, gazing into those beautiful hazel eyes. This stranger looked deep into his heart and saw what was there, yet he responded with compassion and understanding. It was confusing and jarring at the same time.

He lowered his face. He couldn't look into those eyes with the shame he felt creeping into his heart. Who was this man who stood before him?

"I see the hurt inside you," Elihu repeated as he placed a hand on Anan's shoulder, speaking ever so gently. "Come, Anan. Let us go back to your father's house, together."

Anan lifted his eyes to this stranger and whispered, "Lord?"

# CHAPTER TWENTY-TWO

## *Kadesh*

Attilius held his wife's hand in his as he looked down in shame. They were sitting at the table, all of them together. He had asked his wife and daughter to come and sit with him so they could talk. They had complied, but hesitantly.

He looked into Cloelia's face, tears welling up in her eyes. "I know I've hurt you," he said, "and I'm so very sorry."

His voice wavered as he chose his words carefully. Apologizing didn't come easy to him. In all his life, this may have been his first apology.

"I have neglected you, both of you," he added, turning to Cassia. "I should have protected you. I should have cared for you more. I shouldn't have let the failings of the farm affect how I treated you. I am so very sorry."

His voice broke. The ache in his chest was smothering.

He looked again at his daughter, sitting quietly across from him, arms crossed in front of her, eyeing him with skepticism.

"Cassia, my daughter, I'm sorry. I didn't recognize what my uncle was doing. I just didn't see it. His behavior towards you was deplorable and I should have protected you. He treated both of you shamefully. I'm so very sorry." He squeezed his wife's hand gently. "Please forgive me."

The room fell silent as his eyes dropped shamefully to her delicate hand in his.

"Attilius," whispered his wife. Cloelia was unsure of her husband's change of heart. Was this authentic? "We love you and we've missed you. You have changed from the man I married so many years ago. You've become harsh and cynical. I feared your uncle had changed you forever."

"I know, I know," Attilius agreed remorsefully.

She studied his face carefully, then rested a second dainty hand on top of his, cupping his large workworn hands between hers.

"But I see you are truly sorry," she continued. "Yes, of course you are forgiven, my dear husband. Of course."

She stood up and stepped towards him, wrapping her arms around his shoulders. He pulled her into himself to bury his head in her belly as he wept.

Cassia blandly watched her parents, arms still crossed. She had felt numb ever since her father's uncle had come into her room. It still made her sick to think about it. Yes, her father was supposed to have protected her but hadn't. She searched her heart for any slip of forgiveness, but there was none to be found. It just wasn't there. Only a deep, numbing anger.

A sudden knock at the door gave Cassia the excuse to slip out of her seat and away from her parents and this awkward show of affection.

She opened the door to see a young man standing before her. She opened the door wide for her parents to see who it was. She didn't recognize the man, but maybe her parents did.

"Aziel?" Attilius asked, bewildered.

Attilius stood up, feeling confused as he stared at his worker from just a few weeks ago, now cleaned up and dressed in new clothes. The young man's dark hair was neatly combed and curled away from his face. Attilius saw what his face truly looked like, clean and shaven.

"Aziel…" He wiped tears from his face with his sleeve. "I owe you for weeks of work. I don't have much, but I will pay your wages as best I can… and if you need work, I will gladly take you back. Again, I don't have much, but I will pay you…"

"No, no, Attilius, I'm not here for wages or for work." Aziel smiled at the family excitedly. He stepped aside, allowing Gamaliel to step forward into the room. "I want you to meet my father…"

CONCLUSION

## *Come Back to Your Father's House*

The story of the prodigal son speaks to us in different ways, depending on our experiences and where we are in our lives. Throughout this book, you have read about the deep hurt that can exist within a family because of personal decisions or the choices of others. Each of us can relate to many, if not all, the characters in the book in different seasons of our lives.

I've titled this book *I Am the Prodigal, I Am the Eldest* because I see myself in both characters. I was a difficult teenager for my parents and have been distant from God in different seasons in my life. But I was also the one in church who scowled at the brother who sat beside me with a shaved head, tattoos, and earrings.

Maybe you relate to either, or both, of the two brothers.

## *The Prodigal*

You may feel like Aziel, the youngest son. You may have wanted adventure, to go and see the world and experience new challenges and opportunities. Yet the ways of the world dragged you into something deep, dangerous, unexpected, and now overwhelming. And no matter how much you try to claw your way out of the influences of the world, the communities and distractions you've associated with continue to drag you back, and you aren't strong enough to turn away.

You may have been overtaken by the influences of drugs and drinking, prostitutes and pornography, fraud, theft, or vandalism. Perhaps you are living a life for sheer pleasure and self-indulgence, and nothing more.

But here you are, reading about Aziel and Halal, both wanting to experience the world at its finest, yet they saw the world for its hate, violence, and ultimate destruction. Aziel returned home; Halal lived and died in his shame.

Please know, dear reader, that God can meet you where you are. Your heavenly Father loves you more than you could ever imagine and wants to see you be free from addiction, the bondage of reckless and destructive living. He is the way out of that self-destructive world. He is the ultimate Healer, the only way out, the One who can break the chains that bind you. He wants to bless you more than you could ever imagine. He is an extravagant Father and wants to love you extravagantly! He can cover the filth in your life with His anointing blood that cleanses you of your past, just like Gamaliel covered Aziel with his robe to hide the world's stench and filth from the very community that was ready to reject him.

Not only is your heavenly Father able to do this, but He *wants* to. You are no longer a slave to the world's self-destructive temptations when you wear your Father's shoes of peace and wholeness. He gives you His signet ring to claim authority through His Son and Holy Spirit. How extravagant is that!

## *The Eldest*

You may be like the older son, Anan, who does everything right according to the commandments. You have respected your parents and followed their lead in living a righteous life. You have tried to raise your family in a godly way, attended church regularly, participated or even led Bible studies, taught Sunday school, and led at ministerial events.

And yet there is no joy in what you do. The conflicts in the church and the gossip and backstabbing of fellow believers have sucked the joy out of your calling. At one time you attended church and rejoiced with your brothers and sisters in Christ, singing to the heavens, thrilled when a new soul came to Christ to sit beside you in the pews and praise Jesus with you together in adoration.

Instead of rejoicing, you now look at them with sarcasm, criticism, and judgment. You focus on the earrings and tattoos, the black leathers and biker boots, instead of the raised hands of a repentant believer who is rejoicing in the love of Jesus, being found by the True Shepherd who came looking for him. Instead of thankful praise, you're filled with cynicism.

Dear reader, know that Jesus will meet you where you are! If you are the older brother, full of sarcasm and disdain for your fellow brothers and sisters, or for those who are still lost and have yet to be found, He can return that accepting and joyful spirit to your soul. He can replace the jealousy and anger you feel with His unconditional love and forgiveness.

He can meet you where you are! Jesus is like your older brother and wants you to truly see the Father's heart, full of love and mercy. He is forever faithful and calls you back to Him. Ultimately, He wants you to be like Aziel, who introduces his father to someone who needs to meet Him!

## *The Waiting Parent*

You may be like Gamaliel, raising your children to love, respect, and follow God, to claim Jesus as their Savior and the Holy Spirit as their Guide. You have taught them scripture and all the wonderful joys of His Word, but also passed on all the somber warnings of a sordid lifestyle. Through breathtaking nature and the incredible beauty in the world, in the sea and in the sky, you've shared the extravagance of God the Creator. You've taught them of the love of Jesus, His ultimate sacrifice, and His acceptance and forgiveness as Redeemer.

And yet the world called your child away and they never looked back. Your heart breaks for them every day, longing for their return.

You may be like Gamaliel and Ednah, still waiting for your child to come home. You persistently petition the throne of Jehovah for them. Your eyes search for them everywhere you go, thinking that perhaps today you might catch a glimpse of them in a parking lot, or at the grocery store. You beg your heavenly Father to hear your pleas—not just to listen, but to respond, so that maybe one day your child, whom you haven't seen in years, or your grandchildren, whom you've never met, will come home to your aching arms.

Dear mother or father, Jesus meets you where you are. He knows the love in your heart. He knows the ache in your arms. He sees your tears on their birthdays, the empty chair at Christmas, and the boxes of memories in the closet. Know that He is working in their lives as well. He has not abandoned them but continues to call them home to Him.

Jesus is like *their* older brother. He is calling them home through His Holy Spirit. Don't give up. Keep advocating for your children. Pray blessings on them before the Lord! Know that as much as you love your children and grandchildren to the core of your being, the Lord loves them even more. Is it possible that another could love them more than you? Yes—your heavenly Father and Jesus His Son does!

## *The Broken Child*

You may be like Cassia, the young girl whose uncle sat outside her door waiting for her. You may be that girl or boy who realized too late that you were being watched by someone you trusted, but they were not worthy of your trust. Instead they were watching you with lustful eyes as you matured and grew into a young adult.

That family member, neighbor, or friend may have done more than just wait outside your door. Your innocence may be gone forever. You blame yourself for their actions towards you, yet it was they who manipulated the situation for their own benefit and twisted desire. You paid the price and now you are caught in a web of self-loathing.

Dear child of God, Jesus meets you where you are! He knows the pain, anger, and disgust you feel in your gut. He weeps with you as you remember the horrible things others have done. Your parents were supposed to protect you but didn't recognize those dangers directed at you. Or maybe they were distracted by their own struggles. He is dealing with them in His own way, but you don't have to suffer anymore.

Know that Jesus died on the cross for your sins, yes, but also for the sins and ugliness that others have inflicted on you. His blood covers all of it. He is like your older brother and calls you home to your heavenly Father to be held and loved as a child of His who was never supposed to be hurt like this.

Jesus meets you where you are in this broken world. He can heal your broken spirit that feels hopeless. He can heal those horrible memories that haunt you, the broken heart that aches so much that you can hardly breathe. He can heal the fears that terrorize you, the overwhelming sorrow that drowns you, and the loss of that sweet childish innocence that was taken from you.

He can make you whole again! He *wants* to make you whole again. Give Him your hurts. Lay them down at the foot of His cross. Accept His healing hands and ask Him for a renewed heart.

## *The Aching Mother*

You may be like the mother who didn't know her child was being pursued or made a target by a family member or friend. You saw the changes in your child. They went from being carefree and affectionate to being silent and withdrawn, like something inside of them had broken. You can't understand how you missed all the cues, how someone you trusted could do that kind of thing to your beautiful child. You have such regret and shame for allowing it to happen, even though you didn't know.

Now you carry that shame and regret and sadness with you every single day. You own the statement "A mother is as happy as her saddest child." You've talked to your child and apologized. You've tried to make things right and get them help and support in their brokenness, but your child is damaged and hurt and it feels like you can't do anything to help except lift them up in prayer.

Dear parent, Jesus meets you where you are! As a parent, you feel like a failure. But know that your heavenly Father loves you more deeply than you can imagine, and He wants you to be released from that pain and regret and shame that consumes you. Know that He is speaking to your child and drawing that child into His arms. He knows their story—all of it! He wants to see them healed and whole, as much and more than you.

Continue to bring your child before the throne of the Great Physician through your prayers and petitions. He hears you and sees your pain as the parent of a broken child, and the pain of that broken child. He knows both sides of this painful experience and wants to bring healing to both of you. He will meet you where you are.

## *The Prodigal Still Lost*

You may be like Halal, the prodigal who never returned. Through circumstances beyond your control, mixed with unwise decisions and poor choices, you have lost everything you knew and cared about. All you have left is a broken spirit. You played on the devil's courtyard and lost your self-respect, sense of self, and purpose and meaning. You may have lost your family and the close relationships you held most dear at one time.

Jesus has come to you so many times, and in so many ways, through church members or friends, through music by way of a song that calls you back to your heavenly Father's arms, through a child of your own who begs you to return to His calling and become a righteous parent, or through a TV or radio program. But your shame and stubbornness have kept you from coming back into your Father's arms. You've lived a life of regret for so many years.

Know that Jesus meets you where you are as a child of God, right now! Nothing can separate you from the love of God—not your shame, not your guilt. However, if you continue down the path of destruction, you will wander further and further away from your Father. How can He help you when your face is turned away from Him?

Return to the One who loves you, who *wants* to bless you with His extravagance! He wants to love you like you deserve to be loved. Your heavenly Father waits for you with open arms. His love for you is never-ending, always pursuing, always available, and deeper than any human being could ever love another.

Have you been led to read this book? Does it tug at your heart to come back to your Father's house? His arms are always open and He's always watching for your return. He is your heavenly Father who loves you so very much!

But I also want you to know, dear reader, that Jesus is your brother. Yes, He is the elder brother, God's firstborn who left everything, a life of extravagance, to go out and find you in a cruel and broken world. He is calling you now. It doesn't matter where you are in life or which season you're in. He wants to meet you where you are!

Return to your Father's house. Come back to Him and be forgiven and healed and blessed by Him. Turn your face towards your Father, because He will meet you wherever you are. That is just one of His many promises.

## *The Longing Wife*

You may be like Cloelia, recognizing the changes in your husband as his friends or family influence him away from you and your family. This man sitting across from you at the breakfast table is not the dear husband you married so many years ago. You share a house but are only roommates.

Raising your children is your common goal, but the together-ness is gone. Marriage is a covenant between you, your husband, and God. Your heavenly Father designed marriage as a way for two people to complete each other—to be a blessing to both. It's sup-posed to be the most intimate relationship here on earth, second only to one's relationship with Jesus and our heavenly Father.

Dear sister in Christ, Jesus will meet you where you are. He knows your longings as a woman to be truly cherished by your husband, to be his absolute delight, to be his soulmate as no other person can be for him. Give this to your loving Father, the One who created marriage in all its wonder and intimacy!

## *The Farmer*

Finally, you may be like the wealthy farmer, Attilius, thinking that you're working hard for your family. And yet you find yourself separated from them. By working long hours, you thought you were providing everything they needed. However, you forgot to give them yourself—your love, your affection, and your attention—and now you recognize that you've lost your family, self-respect, sense of self, and perhaps your job and sense of purpose. Everything you knew and cared about, all that you once had, is gone. All that's left is your broken spirit and broken relationships.

If you are that man or woman, dear friend, then Jesus meets you where you are. You may never have met Jesus your Savior in all His forgiveness, in all His acceptance and love. Give your life to Him today.

The Bible says that if you confess to Jesus your need of Him, acknowledge that you're a sinner, and ask for forgiveness, and if you believe that He is the Son of God and died for your sins on the cross, that He was raised from the dead, then you too can become a child of God and live with Him in eternity. All you have to do is declare Him as Lord and Savior by giving Him your heart. If you pray this in Jesus's name, all of heaven shouts, "Amen!"

As the apostle Luke writes,

> I tell you that in the same way there will be more rejoicing in heaven over one sinner who repents than over ninety-nine righteous persons who do not need to repent...
>
> In the same way, I tell you, there is rejoicing in the presence of the angels of God over one sinner who repents. (Luke 15:7, 10, NIV)

Now, believer, go out and share this good news with others, like Aziel did in sharing the love of his father with his master, Attilius. Spend time with your Bible and read about the extravagance of His creation, the wonder of Christ's birth, the solid teaching of Jesus, the calling of His disciples, His ugly death on the cross, and His glorious resurrection.

Jesus is coming back for His own—to bring us to His heavenly Father's mansion in all His extravagance. He will call you by name, dear brother and sister, because He knows you and waits for you to come home. Jesus is the Prodigal Son and the Eldest Brother!

This is my prayer for you, dear reader:

For this reason I bow my knees to the Father of our Lord Jesus Christ, from whom the whole family in heaven and earth is named, that He would grant you, according to the riches of His glory, to be strengthened with might through His Spirit in the inner man, that Christ may dwell in your hearts through faith; that you, being rooted and grounded in love, may be able to comprehend with all the saints what is the width and length and depth and height—to know the love of Christ which passes knowledge; that you may be filled with all the fullness of God.

Now to Him who is able to do exceedingly abundantly above all that we ask or think, according to the power that works in us, to Him be glory in the church by Christ Jesus to all generations, forever and ever. Amen. (Ephesians 3:14–21)

For God so loved the world that He gave His only begotten Son, that whoever believes in Him should not perish but have everlasting life. (John 3:16)

But God demonstrates His own love toward us, in that while we were still sinners, Christ died for us. (Romans 5:8)

Yes, I have loved you with an everlasting love; therefore with lovingkindness I have drawn you. (Jeremiah 31:3)

Yet to all who did receive him, to those who believed in his name, he gave the right to become children of God—

children born not of natural descent, nor of human decision or a husband's will, but born of God. (John 1:12–13, NIV)

See what great love the Father has lavished on us, that we should be called children of God! And that is what we are! The reason the world does not know us is that it did not know him. Dear friends, now we are children of God, and what we will be has not yet been made known. But we know that when Christ appears, we shall be like him, for we shall see him as he is. All who have this hope in him purify themselves, just as he is pure. (1 John 3:1–3, NIV)